THE WATCHMAN CALLS THE HOURS

THE WATCHMAN CALLS THE HOURS

David Mills

BANKHOUSE

First published in the United Kingdom in 2013 by
Bank House Books
PO Box 3
NEW ROMNEY
UK TN29 9WJ

www.bankhousebooks.com

British Library Cataloguing in Publication Data
A catalogue record for this book is available from the British Library.

ISBN 978-0-9573058-2-3

Front cover photograph: Tony Grist
Design and graphics: Dave Randle
Editor: Simon Fletcher

Typesetting and origination by Bank House Books

This book is dedicated to the memory of my friend Mark Bytheway, one-time World Quiz Champion and Brain of Britain. I would also like to remember Raymond Woodhouse and Jane Carney.

RIP

Chapter One

A fog had risen from the waters around Lichfield Cathedral, mixed, as ever, with soot from fires and muck from the nearby Black Country. The fog filled the Close and made the three spires of the cathedral half distinct. George Bytheway, senior clerk, was on his way home. He often walked home this way but tonight something was different, because somebody screamed. He looked up, feeling his stomach turn over and tried to place the sound. The gas lamps smudged an orange light in the dark and fog, the cathedral stood over him, and then he heard it again and placed it this time. He had never thought of himself as brave, nor was he young, but he ran forward, taking his walking stick like a club in his right hand, his tumbled hat left lying behind him and saw a figure in the dark. The figure in the dark became a woman. He put his hands on her shoulders and she shook as if he had electrified her.

'Good Heavens, what's the matter?'

Bytheway looked straight into her eyes. He had believed her to be fighting for her life but she was alone. She turned to him, a working girl but none the worse for that. As she turned he saw her expression change, and she seemed to collect herself.

1

'What is it?' said Bytheway.

'There was a man,' she said, 'in odd clothing sir, on a horse, and they walked through that wall, just as I looked at them, sir, and he looked at me.'

'Good God,' said Bytheway, turning to look at the solid wall, which curved away to where Dam Street met the Close. 'Good God.' Bytheway forgot himself. 'Good God.'

'I must go, sir,' she said, 'My mother will be missing me.'

'Oh,' he said. 'Yes,' and removed his hands. 'Here'. He produced a shilling, which he gave to her, but did not hear her thanks and only half noticed as she took to her heels, running for home and her mother.

'Good Heavens,' he said softly, and walked up to the wall, putting his hand upon the rough, damp, corporeal bricks. He turned and considered the long, black shape of the cathedral and swept a glance across all the house fronts, all of which had seen this thing, then took to his heels and hurried home, almost running himself.

So it was at the next meeting of the Lichfield Philosophical Club that Bytheway was in great excitement. He was to talk to the club about the apparition, because it meant so much. Mr Darwin's recent book, *On the Origin of the Species*, had shaken belief in God. This ghost story seemed to confound all the doubters.

Doubters had sadly grown in number since *The Origin of the Species*. The book was profound, so much so that it was hard to ignore. This was not to say that Faith was dead but the Church was fighting a rearguard action. So it was that Bytheway was wary. The men might not be receptive to his tale and, in fact, one of the members wanted to crush him. So the stage was set for a confrontation and Bytheway, who was not naturally combative, was caught between his convictions and a slight sense of foreboding.

Given the argument which was brewing, the venue of their meeting was apt, and perhaps some of the more thoughtful men realised this coincidence? Their hall stood where Edward

Wightman had been burned at the stake in 1612. Wightman had died for his faith, for committing a heresy. Such a punishment threw into relief the freedom which they enjoyed in their enlightened age, but also how deeply religion could be felt. Secondly, in the market-place nearby was the statue of Doctor Johnson. Johnson had been a devout Christian, too. He had also been a man of great moral courage, who was prepared to look unpalatable things in the face. Bytheway sometimes wondered what the doctor would have made of the march of science. Would Johnson's faith have withstood the great winds which were now blowing mere striplings to the ground? In his statue the doctor seemed to be pondering the matter, as well he might.

For those yet of flesh and blood there was the meeting to enjoy, seasoned as it might well be by an argument. For some men the merits and demerits of such argument were irrelevant; they anticipated the quarrel itself. For whatever reason, most men were ready before the appointed time and seated five minutes early. What a noisy company they were, too. There were blasts of laughter, low conversation, movement between seats. Up to a point too they rubbed shoulders in a sort of democracy; among working members were gentlemen, who shared in the sense of wonder of that progressive age. Such men wanted to share their learning and lead their fellow men towards the light.

Among the tobacco smoke, and in the chatter and all the anticipation, one man attracted attention more than any other. The eye found him out without intending it. This man was John Deacon, and it was he who waited to oppose Bytheway. Short and portly, Deacon was, none the less, remarkable. The richest man in Lichfield, he was also a man of energy. He experimented with photography, for example; and borrowed animals to study them. He read geology, studied phrenology and seemed to sit on every committee in the city. Mr Deacon was a banker and owned the bank, J.W. Deacon. Mr Bytheway was his clerk.

'Gentlemen, gentlemen.' Mr Rowbotham, in the chair, got to his feet. 'Em-em-em-em.' Mr Rowbotham often em-em-emed. As ever, he looked to the ceiling and his mouth flapped. 'Em, em, we

3

have before us this evening the report of a most singular occurrence. One might scruple to admit such an account in a scientific society, but Mr Bytheway is convinced both of its veracity and absolute importance. Mr Bytheway.'

George Bytheway got to his feet. In his eyes was a kind of light. Indeed, Bytheway was like a Speaker's Corner tub thumper, or a lighthouse, and he shone his light on each of them in turn. Short-haired, with a side parting, dressed smartly, he had a nice face, even and well made. He was the model, too, of mildness and had soft grey eyes, which were almost always benign, but as he looked around the company he radiated excitement, so that they sat up or lent forward, listening properly.

'Gentlemen, last Tuesday evening something happened, not half a mile from here, wondrous in the inference which we may draw from it. Firstly, however, you'll recall that Science proposes that our world is older than the Bible would suggest. The world, we are informed, has changed and changed and changed again. Whole races of animals have undergone extinctions: in short, all we know in the natural world wasn't created once, and once only, as the Bible would suggest, but do not be discouraged! I'll attest to something which proves the survival of the spirit! We may have to read our Bibles differently, without, necessarily, so literal an understanding, but Science must recognise the fundamental underpinning of faith!'

'I doubt that very much!' The voice which made this remark bellowed over the heads. There was some turning round, shuffling. One or two men listened the harder as they sensed a confrontation.

'You're whistling in the dark, whistling in the dark.'

There could be no doubt from where the voice had come. Deacon was wearing an expression like a bulldog. 'Whistling in the dark.' He sat with his arms folded and head squashed into his shoulders as if someone had sat on it. Bytheway reddened; it was difficult for him when his employer took so different a view from his own, but he proceeded.

'Find some moral courage, man,' said Deacon.

'We've all now read, I think,' continued Bytheway, who was visibly shaken, 'Mr Darwin's recent work, *The Origin of Species By Means of Natural Selection?* Mr Darwin is not a Christian, gentlemen; he takes the view that life on this planet has arisen, not as Holy Revelation tells us, but by a result of deductible, discernible laws – natural laws – and that life, life as we know it, in all its variety, has come about by minute changes, age after age, to a common root. I'm not so stupid gentlemen,' Bytheway reddened and his voice became higher, 'that I mistake Mr Darwin's intention. He envisages a natural world which is devoid of God. Can you conceive of a more bleak prospect? For example, consider the descent of Man, as Mr Darwin would have it. Are we not to infer that Mankind shares the same origination as any other animal, that Man is no more than a better sort of beast?'

There was a reaction to this: disagreement, agreement, muffled voices.

Mr Bytheway has explained the matter capitally,' said Deacon loudly, ostensibly talking to Woodhouse, who also worked for the bank. 'I knew that there must be some reason why I continue to employ him.'

Not by word, of course, but by expression, Bytheway seemed irritated by the interruption, but what might he do? He took a sip of water and waited for the attention of the company. In the audience was Carney, who had himself worked in the bank. He was ill and depended upon Faith too much to be indifferent to Deacon. The interruption subsided and Bytheway went on.

'Last Tuesday, last Tuesday of this week, a woman was walking in the Close when she saw an apparition!' Bytheway's eyes shone; this was his trump card. 'Near where Dam Street meets the Close a woman saw a man, a man on a horse. The man took notice of her, looked at her, and then man and horse passed through the wall and disappeared from sight!'

Silence greeted this account; the faces of the men turned to Bytheway. Like naughty boys in class, too, the men also stole glances at Deacon. There was a pause. One might almost have counted the hiatus out: one, two, one two, then Deacon got to his feet.

'There's nothing, Mr Bytheway, but the here and now!' Deacon was declaiming as if from a pulpit. Men in front of him turned round; those obstructed stood up; men craned forward or lent across each other to see. 'Ghosts!' He turned to the men in a gesture which encompassed them all. 'Shall we walk you home tonight? We shall, if you are frightened, George: you and your superstitions, but, forgive me, I grow facetious. This is nonsense, you must see that. Come along, you're whistling in the dark, whistling in the dark, and no more than that.'

'This occurrence proves the survival of the spirit,' insisted Bytheway.

'There is no survival of the spirit!'

'Forgive me, sir,' Bytheway said. He puffed out his chest and stood to his full five feet eleven inches. 'You are mistaken. I know it in my heart.'

'You know it in your heart! I wish that you knew your business in my bank so well. We live and we die, Bytheway. There is no superintending providence, no great design.'

'We see the hand of the Almighty everywhere about us, Mr Deacon, everywhere! You well know, sir, how Mr Paley has compared the work of the Almighty to that of a watchmaker, such is the order of the natural world and the dependence of one part upon another.'

'Nonsense, man!' Deacon was on his feet again but shouting now. 'Consider your chest over that heart of yours, of all the things which I might adduce; have you a nipple? What's the point of that? Have you suckled a child? Could you do so if you so desired? No! Why then did the Almighty give you one and not spare himself the trouble? Shall I tell you why? There is no Almighty and we weren't designed, that is why!'

'That is not so!'

'Em-em-em,' said Rowbotham.

'How you would have contested Copernicus and Galileo.' Deacon pointed a long finger at Bytheway and peered along its length. 'You, sir! Perhaps you still believe that the sun revolves around the earth?'

'You will forgive me, sir ...'

'Gentlemen!' implored Mr Rowbotham.

'But,' continued Bytheway, ' you forget yourself. Fifty yards from here, Edward Wightman died for his faith in 1612. Here in the market-place behind this building! Yet you treat Faith with so little regard.'

'Indeed,' said Deacon icily, 'Perhaps you think ...'

'Gentlemen!' interrupted Rowbotham.

'Perhaps you think,' repeated Deacon, 'That I should burn? I think that you forget yourself, sir! This is 1860, and we've done with your superstitious nonsense! I advise you to mind your tongue.' Deacon was bustling now through the chairs. 'Don't be late in arriving at the bank tomorrow, Mr Bytheway and be careful not to displease me. I'm sick and tired of your crack-brained cant, and I won't stay to listen to another word. You've set aside your judgement, sir, and I'm disgusted by you. Goodnight, gentlemen!'

The last chair was kicked from his way. Deacon picked up his stick, forced his top hat onto his head and barged out, slamming the door behind him. As ever, he left a sort of vacuum behind him. Just as one knew when Deacon was in a room, so one noticed when he left. There was silence once he had gone; for perhaps a minute no one said a word. There was a lame attempt to continue eventually but it came to nothing, the wind had gone from their evening, which had seemed a fair wind. So it was that that meeting of the Lichfield Philosophical Society reached a premature end. The room was empty within ten minutes of Deacon leaving them and they left, talking loudly, but somehow in a great want of spirits.

Chapter Two

The bank of J.W. Deacon had run for nearly twenty-five years and won a reputation for reliability and probity, much of which was thanks to Bytheway. Mr Deacon depended upon Bytheway, and with Deacon's distractions outside the bank, so Bytheway had increasingly managed its affairs. The trust which was placed in him was something which Bytheway treasured. He was paid £400 a year, too: £400 a year, when most people earned much less. His wage was a good one, but much depended on him: the bank managed the accounts of most of Lichfield's tradespeople and gentry.

Bytheway never forgot his good fortune, but was troubled despite it. Bytheway and Deacon had grown apart. Ever since Mrs Deacon's death, Deacon had changed. He now hated the Church, and Bytheway, with his steadfast faith (as Deacon thought), galled him.

The circumstances surrounding Mrs Deacon's illness were mysterious, save that she had produced several dead or short-lived children and finally died herself. Bytheway occasionally pondered her illness but knew better than to mention it. He had once offered Deacon religious consolation: never again!

Consequently, Deacon was not inclined to count his blessings. Indeed, after his wife's death, Deacon's latent atheisim became stronger. Opposition to his opinions also became an offence, and so it was, on the morning after the meeting of the Society, that Bytheway was having to defend his conduct of the night before.

'As it was a matter of conscience, sir, and away from the bank, I felt that I was at liberty to express myself as I did.'

Bytheway, Woodhouse noted, tried for composure, but licked his lips and rubbed his hands too.

'You will not humiliate me publicly,' shouted Deacon. 'How dare you, sir, take issue with me and contradict me!'

Deacon seemed unaware of the humiliation that he inflicted upon Bytheway. One might have expected him to speak privately and not in front of the junior clerk. Perhaps it was a lapse of judgement; perhaps he did not care.

'I have a position in this city: there is good reason why I have been chairman of this, director of that, sit on the Board of Guardians, and so on, and so forgive me if I claim a modicum of respect from you!'

He stopped. As if from the goodness of his soul he looked under his brows at Bytheway. Oh, how he had to have the patience of a saint with his senior clerk! The exertion of shouting had made his cheeks shine and his nose glistened, while the gingery whiskers on his chops looked damp.

Bytheway, as ever, embodied self restraint. With his chin up and back straight he was a gentleman and clung to this idea of himself. Even now he listened with great attention, but a tremor shook one of his legs and he rubbed his hands. Woodhouse, meanwhile, bubbled like a pot on the fire. Bytheway noted Woodhouse, but watched the operation of Deacon's mouth as Deacon began upon something else.

'You need not trouble yourself to dispute with me. A man such as John Deacon will always finish uppermost. Uppermost, George, uppermost! Mark my words, I have a position in this city. Public confidence in this bank is everything, everything. That confidence is vested in me and once that confidence is lost ... I tell you, George ...'

Deacon's teeth and jaw seemed to Bytheway like those of a ventriloquist's dummy until, at last, they stopped. At the end of this chatter the lips and teeth conjoined into a smile, a smile of infinite goodness, and whether it was the condescension or the shouting or the humiliation or whether it was Woodhouse's sniggering but something stirred in Bytheway. Christian as he was, and loyal clerk, he struggled to contain it; his breathing quickened and he had to swallow it, swallow it, but his hand-rubbing gathered pace, and he rubbed and rubbed until Deacon told him to stop it.

'Get about your work,' said Deacon suddenly to Woodhouse. The young man dropped his head at once. 'Keep him to his business, Mr Bytheway.' And with that, which passed for a civil word, he went. Bytheway bowed. Woodhouse scrambled to his feet and bowed too, and then they were left to themselves. As ever, Deacon left a sort of vacuum behind him; it was as if he took away their capacity to act while he was there, and once he was gone it demanded great will to do anything at all. Bytheway, too, had to make a transition from the naughty schoolboy that Deacon had made him seem to senior clerk. This was not easy, and Woodhouse needed little enough encouragement to forget the boundary that existed between them. However, the two clerks adjusted themselves to the sudden alteration. They worked on in silence, each behind a high wooden desk. The pens of each man scratched, and sometimes the thick paper in their ledgers make a noise as one of them turned a page. Bytheway had the feeling, despite the silence, that Woodhouse had something to say. The clock made itself known and intruded upon them. The regular beat of the pendulum seemed to heighten the sense of something unsaid. Despite himself, Bytheway looked at the young man. Woodhouse seemed to suck upon some joke or other and to have trouble containing his thoughts. Bytheway wondered if the joke were at his expense. At the best of times Woodhouse had a sly face, with cocky, knowing eyes, and sometimes, for all that

11

Bytheway tried, Woodhouse's confidence undermined his own. Woodhouse looked up suddenly and caught Bytheway staring at him. The smile broke over the young man's face.

'It seems to happen a lot now, Mr George.'

The chair creaked under Bytheway. He looked towards the daylight seeping in through the windows. The light shone on the polished counter that separated them from their customers. 'Of what do you speak?' Bytheway knew perfectly well what Woodhouse meant.

'Mr Deacon, sir, is always having a cut at you these days.'

'My relationship with Mr Deacon is of no concern to you.' Bytheway tried to be stern.

Woodhouse smiled. 'But it is, Mr George. I hate to see you being upset, sir. I don't like to see him humiliate you, sir.'

A flicker of irritation, divided between Woodhouse and Deacon, rose in Bytheway. 'You are most considerate.'

Woodhouse smiled again and bowed, but raised his eyes and looked at Bytheway. Bytheway put his head down. He attempted to work, but the clock again intruded as the room had become quiet. Bytheway could hear the clock clearly as he listened for Woodhouse; and he was right: Woodhouse had more to say.

'You know, Mr George,' he said, dropping his voice and talking more quickly, 'I've been watching you, sir, and I don't think that you're a happy man. I think I know how you can get some satisfaction, give Mr Deacon some of his own medicine, and make us happy into the bargain.'

What did Woodhouse mean by this? Was he suggesting theft from the bank? The hair stood upon Bytheway's neck. He felt himself turn red. 'Am I to believe my ears?'

'I've been thinking about it for some time now, sir, and I've been watching you. I can see how much Mr Deacon upsets you.'

'Desist,' thundered Bytheway, not wanting to hear one word more. 'I shall go to Mr Deacon, sir. I shall report you!'

'No,' said Woodhouse, keeping his eyes on Bytheway. 'No, sir. I think you've misunderstood me, Mr Bytheway. Don't imagine anything improper! I didn't mean that, sir. I meant that you and me, in our nice little bank, shouldn't let him upset us, and that you should concentrate upon your work and not try so hard to please him. That's what I meant. Mr Deacon's such a bully, sir. It would thrill me to see him unable to trouble you. Please don't say a word to Mr Deacon, sir. I'd lose my position, be cast out. You can't cast me out. I meant nothing improper, sir, really I didn't.'

Bytheway looked at Woodhouse, who coloured and looked guilty, but Woodhouse would later laugh about Bytheway's appearance at that moment; he was open mouthed, with eyes like butterfly nets. The moment passed; at least Woodhouse hoped that it had passed. He switched on his lopsided grin and busied himself about nothing, but Bytheway watched him: he thought that he had understood Woodhouse very well.

So it was that Woodhouse and Bytheway became silent, and they were still quiet when Deacon came back. Bytheway saw Woodhouse glance at him, and noticed Woodhouse's trepidation, although the young man worked assiduously. Deacon too was busy, busy about this, busy about that, but a word from Bytheway would have sacked Woodhouse. Bytheway looked from Woodhouse to Deacon's office and back again, and sometimes Woodhouse glanced at him, but soon afterwards the three men left their work for the night, and only the briefest of courtesies passed between them.

Chapter Three

Horace Arthur Woodhouse, to give him his full name, sat in his lodgings. He lived in Beacon Street, in a couple of ground-floor rooms facing the road. It was Sunday, and he was wearing an open-necked shirt, waistcoat and matching trousers. He wore his work shoes too and a house coat, now a little out of fashion, but he could not afford to be modish. He wore his hair, however, in a fashionable manner, and hoped that his gold watch chain gave him a racy air.

On the bed were a number of magazines, some of them open. Woodhouse loved to read, particularly about the American West, Australia or the wide expanses of Canada. He liked accounts of prospecting for gold, fighting hostile natives and breaking new ground, turning back the forests and wastes. He liked stories about the river boats on the great Mississippi; he liked tales of the new railways and the tough navvies who prepared the ground. He was saving money for an outing on the railway – and had already been on the train to Walsall, where he had drunk in a public house and smoked a cigar. He had also consorted with a prostitute: she had approached him in a pub and taken him outside. He had not enjoyed the experience and had found it embarrassing, but had done it to thumb his nose at all those respectable crones whom he despised so much. Later he had returned to see her again, and had begun to insinuate himself among the people whom she knew, fancying himself as a young man who could move in the shadows, respected in the seedy underworld. When Woodhouse had gone back to the pub and the man behind the bar had nodded at him, it had been among the greatest moments of his life.

This facility of Woodhouse's to live a double life made him think very well of himself. In the bank he could speak cant with the customers, for example. He listened to their petty complaints and asked after their families; he feigned interest in their concerns, while all the time thinking they were old windbags. Conversely, he felt at home in the smoky bars of Birmingham or Walsall, where it was good to be known and wise not to ask too many questions.

Woodhouse's taste in reading indicated something more about his character. In addition to stories of crime and adventure he liked to read about the acquisition of wealth. For a man like him, a superior man, it was only a question of how he acquired wealth. Among so many blockheads, how he could not rise to the top? He did not mind accounts of racy women either, to speak the truth, or of fighting men. In all these things one thing was evident: they embodied the very opposite of a short-of-funds Sunday afternoon in Lichfield.

Woodhouse tossed a magazine aside. He hated to be bored. Although he picked up another journal, for a moment he thought about something else. Indeed, he thought much more than people knew, nor were his thoughts common thoughts. He thought 'great thoughts', he told himself, beyond the wit of the rabble. Religion was a case in point. He had abandoned his own faith, and despised those who maintained belief. He had debunked religion: it was humbug, and even as a child, before Darwin, Woodhouse flattered himself, he had seen through it. Scepticism was all very well, but what had been left to him? Materialism was his solace, if he needed one. Consumption was his god, but scratching beneath the surface he had a bleak philosophy: enjoy what you can when you can, because tomorrow we die. 'Look at poor Carney!' Woodhouse had said, more than once. Carney had always been a decent chap, and look at him now, clinging by his fingers' ends to life while the world went on without him. Woodhouse was determined that he would not be in a similar position, so he wanted to try things, experiment, live: live, because tomorrow you die.

In accordance with that philosophy Woodhouse had purchased a cigar, and he lit it now. He did not like cigars, nor alcohol, but one had to work at these things. As he puffed away, coughing, he looked sly. He was plotting a scheme: to be plain, he intended to rob the bank. It had been a risk sounding out old George: he had thought for a moment that Bytheway had meant to turn him in. However, two things made him feel safe. For some time now he had watched Bytheway and had noticed how Deacon angered him. There was something else too. He did not know for sure, but he guessed that George was suffering a crisis of faith. If this were the case then all well and good; he would do what he could to intensify it. In fact, he had played Deacon and Bytheway like fish on the end of a line. He had made a fool out of Deacon: for a sharp old thing he was very susceptible. For example, Woodhouse had talked with great enthusiasm to him about Bytheway's ghost story, in such a way that Deacon was enraged. That in itself had caused huge tension between Deacon and George. In all, Woodhouse was convinced that Bytheway could be enlisted into his scheme. He, Horace Arthur Woodhouse, was so clever, and although George Bytheway was a strait-laced, honest old stick he had hopes for him. Old George would turn out very well, he was sure.

Chapter Four

Bytheway stood outside the cathedral, where two matching towers stood flanking a decorated screen. For a thousand years this had been a holy site, a place of pilgrimage and refuge distinct from the working city. During that time the building had been restored many times, and it moved him that the edifice had been passed down the generations, like the Word itself.

Just like the Word, the front was not looking its best presently. Time, it seemed, was eroding stone and text alike, but the work went on to restore the cathedral. Mr Gilbert Scott was renewing the structure's interior and would next turn to the outside.

In studying the building, Bytheway was interrupted more than once but always returned to his thoughts. For example, it amused him to think of Tudor times when parishioners had processed to the cathedral, following a man with a cross. Sometimes rival processions had fought to see which group would enter the Close first.

There were so many stories. Bytheway hoped that the cathedral would ride out the new one, that of Mr Darwin and the march of Science. He hoped that Mr Gilbert Scott would make all new and give the cathedral impetus. This hope buoyed his mood, bolstering his moral purpose – and his decision to tell Deacon that they could not trust Woodhouse.

The sorry matter was wearisome and Bytheway lingered, perhaps to put off the moment of reckoning, but he was also drawn towards Deacon's house. He had every reason to feel excited because Mr Deacon had invited him to meet a house guest. The person's identity was not known to him, but Bytheway had prepared for their meeting with the utmost care. He had polished and re-polished his shoes, shaved carefully and left his ablutions until the last moment. He had also practised the correct mode of addressing his betters and, to seed his conversation, thoroughly read *The Times*. Excited as he was, he was relieved too. Despite all the tension between them here was proof of Deacon's regard for him. Here was recognition of the responsibilities that were vested in him, of his standing as chief clerk. Oh, the sun was bright that morning, and Bytheway felt well of himself and better of Deacon than he had done for some time past.

There was a sprinkle of birdsong as Bytheway made his way from the Close, and though he was busy he could not help but listen. The bird was probably a thrush, and somehow it spoke to his heart, so that he was almost happy as he finally moved on. So, making cheerful recognitions of people he knew, he approached Stowe, which lay across the pool, with a curving path between them. Over the pool was St Chad's Church, stubby, sandy-coloured, and behind it lay Deacon's home. What a fine place it was: a grand old lady of a house, Georgian, red bricked, with white stone at the windows and notched white quoins at the corners.

Bytheway raised a hand to shade his eyes and studied the building. His sight was good and he was discerning too, noting, for example, its old trees. The trees seemed to throw out their arms, like actresses drawing attention to the property. Between the trees was a rising path, and the path and pointing trees brought the visitor to a central door. All in all, the closer one looked at it, or approached it, the more impressive it became.

Bytheway smiled; he could hear his breathing now, not through exertion but in excitement. He returned to the thought that Deacon held him in considerable esteem. However, he must beg time to tell Deacon about Woodhouse. Before this day was out, Woodhouse would be given his notice.

The bell jangled at the door. Hearing it, a shiver of excitement ran through Bytheway. Dr Johnson and Boswell had come here; Thomas Day's attempt to train a perfect wife had been based here. So many people had called, but those who counted had stood where he did now. He did not go round to the rear, as a servant would, but stood proudly at the front, where Dr Johnson had before him.

'George.'

Bytheway spun round, and there was Deacon. He looked jolly enough. He wore a lounge suit, the jacket with narrow cuffs and high-set buttons, which was fashionable for the provinces. His square-toed shoes gleamed and his whiskers were spruce and gingery, like the ruff of a tomcat. Bytheway bowed.

'Come here, George'.

Deacon seemed excited about something: there was a flush on his round-ended nose and cheeks, which made him look like the policeman in a Punch and Judy show.

There was something odd about this. Bytheway had expected to enter the house. He had almost had his foot in the door, believing Deacon, genial as he seemed, was about to usher him inside, but instead Deacon studied him for a moment. 'You know I value your opinion,' he said. His face was round and good natured but serious too, and he put his chin down for gravitas. Bytheway was intrigued, and waited for him to go on.

'My guest,' said Deacon, 'I'd very much like to know your estimation of her. Would you do that, George? I'd be most grateful.'

'Yes, of course.' Bytheway was like a dog with two tails, if truth be told. He was mightily pleased. Deacon clearly valued his judgement more than he had realised. Indeed, Bytheway flattered himself that he was perceptive. He had insight into people, and while he was diffident he was not stupid. Bytheway could not help it, but even indulged in a momentary boast, reminding Deacon about a dishonest customer in the bank whom Bytheway had suspected immediately. When Deacon remembered the incident and praised him anew, Bytheway glowed like a pie taken fresh from the oven.

'Good man,' said Deacon, and clapped him on the back. 'Good man.'

Still they stood outside the house in the bright cheerful day, in view of all the many windows, with the large trees standing round.

'Ah!' Deacon remembered. 'My guest. Do you know that she is distantly related to you? Yes!'

'Really?'

'Yes!'

Bytheway was astonished and very excited now, frankly. A great person related to him and known to Mr Deacon. 'Might I ask her name, Mr Deacon?' In their society patronage counted hugely; family links, however slight, could lead to preference and advancement, as well as respect and social standing. These things mattered in a world where a person stood upon his own merits and state provision for the poor was a short remove from destitution.

'May I meet her, Mr Deacon?'

Deacon smiled: what a tease he could be. He tormented Bytheway a moment longer, smiling a smile, eyes brimming, cheeks as if someone had polished them.

'Come along,' he said finally. At last! thought Bytheway. He picked his chin up and tried to compose himself, although his heart was racing a little now. 'Dignity,' he said to himself, 'Dignity. Be respectable. Be composed!'

Deacon led Bytheway round the house, past some of the extensions on the side of the building. Was the great personage walking in the gardens, perhaps? There was no guest in the gardens, however, only a few workers, who kept their heads down as Deacon approached. Deacon kept on, and came to the stables in the rear which adjoined the servants' quarters. This was very odd. Bytheway could not account for it. Deacon pushed open a wooden door.

'Here, George, is the guest whom I mentioned to you, and a distant cousin of yours, I believe.' He laughed a jolly laugh, and by a gesture of his eyes and brows indicated for Bytheway to follow him. There was a cobbled floor, a strange smell, which was not pleasant, and the din of some raucous animal. The light was subdued and Bytheway had to adjust to it, which he did, although he was aided in seeing by a skylight overhead. Deacon stood aside, and then an animal extended an arm through a cage. It was an ape.

'What is this?' Bytheway was astonished. He looked askance at the jolly face of Deacon. 'My cousin? My cousin, Mr Deacon?'

He felt the lick of anger in him. Deacon was laughing at him. Bytheway remembered an occasion at school when he had struggled with some sum and all the class had laughed, so much so, as his confusion grew, that the boys were rolling at their desks and only the teacher's cane had subdued them. So he felt now, but he swallowed it, swallowed it.

'You know that I'm very fond of my animals,' said Deacon cheerfully. 'She's an orang utang, not mine, but come to live with me for a holiday, one might say. I mean to observe her. I'd like you to observe her too.'

'My cousin,' said Bytheway.

'Yes', said Deacon, 'Your cousin – and mine, George. Now, observe her.'

The ape regarded them with huge and most expressive eyes. She was a ginger colour, heavily built, with great arms and lesser legs. Her lips were incredibly dexterous, and as Deacon pushed some foodstuff through her cage she took it nimbly with soft brown hands, broke it – Deacon called this 'breaking bread' – and manipulated the pieces with her lips before eating them. She was named Maggy, and as Deacon called her name she looked up at

23

him. The ape seemed to understand him. It seemed that she had a considerable intellect.

Bytheway was shocked at Deacon's purpose in inviting him there. To invite him there to humiliate him; it was outrageous! He wondered if he should turn on his heels and go. As Bytheway looked at the ape Deacon watched him, wearing a sort of grin, his eyes lit in merriment. He looked, thought Bytheway, like a boy after a prank. When Deacon lifted a hand, wearily Bytheway followed the gesture, knowing that the game was entering another phase.

'What do you notice about her, George?'

Bytheway scratched his forehead and sighed. None the less he looked at the animal. The ape did have most expressive, intelligent eyes. He said something about her eyes.

'What else? What conclusions may we draw from consideration of this ape?'

'Perhaps you would be so good,' said Bytheway, 'as to tell me?'

Deacon was flinty at this. 'I shall! You may discern her very human features. You must concede that she is, essentially, an animal little different from us. Now, George, I have primed you: what else may we conclude?'

Bytheway folded his arms, looked at the floor and said nothing.

'Come, come, do not be so obtuse. I shall tell you, then. You may adduce from this that Man was not uniquely made in the image of God, but is an animal improved, and so, dear George, we may conclude that each species was not made distinct and immutable. This ape and you, George, are of one clay, except that we have evolved further from our common root.'

'Has she a moral sense?' asked Bytheway. He turned to face Deacon, growing flushed, beginning to speak quickly. Deacon saw this and smiled. 'Has she a soul? Has she a soul?'

'I rather think not,' said Deacon. 'You know, George, I find myself in sympathy with Mr Hume, that the Almighty is a creation of the human mind. You ask about her moral sense. We have no moral sense, other than that imbued in us by our own development as a social animal.'

'No!' declared Bytheway. 'I know otherwise, sir. I know in my heart.'

'You know nothing!' Deacon was bullish now. 'Tears at bedtime, George, tears at bedtime! All arguments for a continued existence after death are fallacious, humbug, and no more than that. People like you, George, take your desire for a life after death as evidence of it.'

'Why?' asked Bytheway, thoroughly angry, barely containing himself, 'why do you say this to me? Why? Is it not monstrous that you seek to rob me of my faith? Monstrous! What have I done to deserve this treatment?'

'You ask me that! When my wife died, after all my children, I could not bear the cant which you offered me. Consolation! Do you know how you tortured me? That the Almighty had some purpose in taking them? That I should accept their loss gladly. Do you know how I miss them? Why might it be, George, that I occupy my time as I do, sitting on every committee in Lichfield, doing so much for the public good? Why? Is it because I am a Christian like you: no! I cannot think of them when I keep myself busy, that is why, and if I devote myself to public works perhaps some good may come of it; there is nothing else to hope for. That is why!'

For a moment Deacon's face crumpled like a scrunched up paper bag. Bytheway noted the screwed-up eyes of his employer, the crow's feet scoring his face. Bytheway had been angry, but felt his anger grow slack and even began to search for some form of words to soften Deacon's distress, but as Bytheway bent down to Deacon and started to console him, Deacon's face became angry. He almost laid hands on Bytheway. He was white-eyed. 'You may believe what you please, but I shall never, never cease from tormenting you, just as you tormented me.'

Bytheway was pinned against the rough wall. He did not know what to say and he suddenly pulled himself away. He felt Deacon's hand on his sleeve but rushed out. The door flew back on its hinges and he rushed out, out into the day. He thought that he heard a remark – conciliatory, perhaps – behind him, but he rushed out and on, round the outside of the house, along the drive and down the path to the road, and at the road raced onto the path beside the pool and on from there. He did not stop running, despite all the people on the path who looked at him, until he reached the precincts of the cathedral, and there he put his head against the rough stone wall, somewhere near where the ghost was reputed to have appeared, and readily might he have wept. Only then did Bytheway realise that he had said nothing about Woodhouse, but, as he set off for home, he hardly felt inclined to mention it, now or later.

Chapter Five

Bytheway and Carney were in the Close. Carney, wrapped up, sat in an invalid chair with Bytheway behind him. It was past midnight and a cold wind blew. The wind fingered inside their clothing and sometimes lifted their hair. Sometimes it seemed to run the back of its fingers down their cheeks, all of which was appropriate as Bytheway and Carney were ghost hunting.

Above the spires, the stars were shining and the heavens were lit. The stars hung aloft, some brighter, some fainter, while a big moon drifted among the clouds. It was a night for spirits, and once, almost like ghosts themselves, they slipped into the shadows when someone chanced by. In the dark the footsteps of the interloper seemed loud, rising and then fading away. And so they hid themselves from time to time, but mostly they wandered, like lost souls one might have said.

' Do you know,' said Carney, softly, 'Mr Deacon called to comfort me on Wednesday night. He was kind enough to bring me a gift. Do you know what that gift was? He'd paid Mr Blackstock, the undertaker, to attend me, once I'm dead of course! How considerate! I could barely refrain from saying, "Mr

Deacon, you shouldn't have!"' Carney gave a little chuckle. 'He had some words of comfort for me, too. "Don't worry, Carney," he said, "You won't know that you're dead!"' Carney laughed, so jolly that one might have thought that he was well. Bytheway laughed too, and chided Carney for ingratitude.

"'I hope that it may be of some consolation to you,"' said Carney, impersonating Deacon, "'that your remains will moulder away in the ground and come to nourish the soil. There, I trust that I have brought some comfort to you!"'

Carney laughed again, and Bytheway joined him. For a moment it was as if they were both well and happy; just for a moment or so.

Their circuit of the Close began and ended where the ghost was reported to have passed through the wall. Both men laid hands on the wall. It was so solid! The damp made their hands ache as they lent on it. So it was that they decided upon a plan. It was Carney's idea. 'Let us hide ourselves in the shadows and surprise this ghost.'

Nearby was a shadow cast by a wall, under the shade of a tree too. The friends withdrew into the darkest dark and waited. Sometimes they watched the wall avidly, sometimes they pretended to look elsewhere, but the ghost was a wily ghost. Suddenly, however, they realised that another person was standing near them. Then a figure appeared in the entrance to the Close. Bytheway felt his breathing shorten. Poor Carney. It would have been funny, but Carney sat transfixed. The man stood near them. They heard his boots scrape on the ground. Once he muttered something, and almost together they realised that it was someone they knew: PC Wagstaff! For a moment their relief, mixed with disappointment, almost gave them away. How might they possibly have explained what they did there in the dark. He was a canny man too, PC Wagstaff, and they had a feeling that he sensed something. All chest and creaky boots, he passed to and fro near them, so near! They held their breath, and eventually heard him walk away in the dark.

It was a strange thing, but as the policeman walked away they both stifled a impulse to call out. Neither told the other about this odd thought, but to both of them Wagstaff represented something vital. He belonged to the world of stolid good sense, clip on the ear justice, three or four sugars in a mug of steaming tea. In leaving them he took that evocation of the day with him, and abandoned them to the dark.

'Cold as the grave,' said Carney softly. 'Cold as the grave.'

At length, the cold drove them out of their recess. Under a tree in darkness beside a damp wall was no place for flesh and blood, and so, while the people of the Close slept, Bytheway and Carney wandered outside. As they went one wheel of the invalid chair squeak-squeaked, squeak-squeaked, squeak-squeaked. This comic noise was almost the only sound made between them. Had the ghost appeared would they have even seen it?

What was beyond doubt, it seemed, if people have any sense of these things, was that this was a night for spectres. There was a high moon running and shadows lying deep. The chill in the air, too, augmented their sense of mortality, but nothing and no one stirred. The ghost wall was so mundane, too. Whenever they approached it their breathing shortened but it was commonplace. None the less, round they went again. At each new beginning they disappeared into the night, until, some minutes later, that noise came again: squeak-squeak, squeak-squeak and they appeared again out of the dark.

Occasionally, almost out of embarrassment, they had snatches of conversation and even shared a jest – but the truth was that they were both miserable. Carney attempted to keep up his spirits but subsided under the weight of private thoughts, and Bytheway was no brighter. He became so lost in reflection that he almost forgot their purpose. 'Splendour in the grass,' he muttered. 'Splendour in the grass.'

Bytheway was thinking of his childhood, when he had come to worship with his mother in the cathedral. During his boyhood God had been as tangible as the people sitting alongside him in the pew. At his mother's knee he had imbibed Bible stories, and

29

the stories had been real to him. At home and school, at work and rest, his life had revolved around his faith, and his faith had centred upon this place. His belief had never been in question; indeed, he had felt a personal relationship with God, and knew the mystery of prayer being answered. Now these early wonders had faded. There was a voice in him that cried as loudly as ever for the Lord, but any response eluded him. Perhaps he had grown worldly, he thought; or perhaps his prayers had centred too much upon himself. For whatever reason, a worm had eroded his iron certainty; but more than this he sensed that the times were changing. He sometimes felt like a watchman calling the hours, marking out time as Science made inroads into everything: challenging, inventing, disproving. In recent years the very ground on which he stood had shaken. How could he believe any longer in the age of the earth as explained by Scripture when Mr Lyell had shown the antiquity of the planet? Nor was the Creation story credible in the light of Darwin's book. Nor could he believe that Man was made in God's image when Man had evolved and not been made, as Darwin suggested.

Thus it was that Bytheway found himself waiting for a spectre to show itself, to prove that the spirit survived death; to prove that the Church, his faith, this cathedral, everything religious was not based on a fallacy or a pretence, and was more than a tune whistled on a dark night.

The thought that there might be nothing but materialism was a miserable one. Bytheway saw the love of money in other people and did not like it. He was disgusted, too, by sensuality. The most elevated moments of his life, the most beautiful, when he had been least like an animal, had come to him through faith. More than anything else, though, his faith gave him hope: hope for himself, hope for poor Carney, hope for everyone he loved or had ever loved, a hope that looked beyond death. There was also something beautiful beyond words in the answers that came to prayer, in the hand that stole into his, in the sense of a power beyond himself that was infinitely good.

For these and other reasons Bytheway could not bear

Deacon's attacks upon his faith, which tortured him in the way that a slug writhes when it has been dipped in salt. He did not know how much longer he could withstand Deacon: sooner or later he would do something desperate, although what this might be he did not know. So it was that it was timely, or untimely, that Carney chose the moment to speak.

'George,' he said, 'be wary of Woodhouse! I think he means to steal from the bank. He came to sit with me, but talked only of you and the cancelled notes. I think he intends to ask your help. Be careful! Tell Mr Deacon: it's only right and proper that you do so. Mr Woodhouse has brought this upon himself. Indeed, I almost told Mr Deacon myself, but I am ill and did not want the trouble of it. I knew I had to tell you instead.'

'Goodness me,' said Bytheway, his stomach turning over. 'Goodness me. Goodness me.'

'What will you do?'

Whether or not Bytheway heard Carney he did not answer; nor did Carney ask again.

The friends spent another few minutes wandering in the Close, waiting and walking, but there were no spectres that night. Finally they stood before the mighty west front and looked at it. The two towers, the gable between them, were blank in the darkness. The friends looked at the building as they would an old friend whom they hardly recognised, and who did not know them. Finally, without a word, they turned, and went home to their beds.

Chapter Six

Bytheway was silent when Deacon entered the bank. He rose, of course, to bow, but said nothing, and Deacon bridled somewhat. Woodhouse, as ever, was alert to the merest friction between them. The men stood looking at each other.

'Get to your work,' said Deacon. The young man dropped like a stone, but Bytheway remained standing. He considered Deacon, who seemed to him like a taunting ginger tomcat on a wall. As Bytheway considered Deacon, so Deacon considered him, like a farmer perusing stock at a cattle market. Caught between deference and irritation, Bytheway stood tall, lifting his nose with a slightly injured air and radiating pride, injured pride. The colour grew in Deacon's cheeks but finally he smiled.

'Come, come, George. I've had to have words with you before.'

'Yes, sir. You've a right to talk to me about the bank.'

Deacon shook his head, and his round face was forgiving, nay generous. 'I'm sorry about our being at crossed purposes. You see, I've apologised! Goodness me, there was no occasion for the manner in which you left. We might have agreed to differ, but I'm not a vengeful man and I'd like to make peace with you. Would you please call at my house on Sunday afternoon at two sharp? I mean to present you with a picture of yourself, a daguerreotype. You know how fond I am of taking daguerreotype images. What can be the harm in that? Will you come?'

Bytheway thought about it. He had been duped before.

'Come along!'

'Forgive me, Mr Deacon, but why do you wish to make an image of me?'

'As a gift. I told you that.'

Bytheway thought, the cogs and wheels turning in his mind.

'Come on, George.'

'Very well, sir; thank you.'

'Good man,' said Deacon, beaming. 'I'll take at least two images and you shall choose the one that you like best.'

'I will admit', said Bytheway, brightening, 'that I would like to have a daguerreotype of myself.'

'Good man!'

A gentleman always keeps his word, and so that Sunday Bytheway found himself on the path to Stowe. For a moment he lingered on the margin of the Close, where a long view presented itself of Deacon's home, which was charming. The house called to him, as always, then best foot forward, and on he went.

It was significant to him that had his father called there, in his day, he would have gone to the rear. Bytheway went to the front door. He was received and entered the house, which was promising. He was almost bright upon meeting Deacon.

'Good afternoon, sir.'

'Come,' said Deacon.

Their footsteps made a sort of conversation until Deacon stopped outside a door. 'Go in.'

Bytheway entered and could not believe his eyes. 'Goodness,' he said, seeing the equipment. 'Hush,' said Deacon; but Bytheway would have struggled to converse. The room stank of chemicals: no, more than stank.

Mr Deacon now turned to prepare something, ignoring Bytheway, who took the opportunity to look round. Where to begin? The walls were bright; there was a camera on a tripod and a bath, heated from beneath by a lamp. There was also a chair opposite the camera, and Deacon, as though moving luggage, suddenly bundled Bytheway into the seat.

It took some effort, but Bytheway settled, although he was obliged to do so. In any case, Deacon was ready. Deacon began polishing a silver-coated copper plate, stroking it in a criss-cross manner, but stopped to beckon a servant.

'Come,' said Deacon. A woman entered carrying a book, which she opened. 'The exposure time is rather drawn out and the chair, I know, isn't altogether comfortable,' said Deacon, 'so I hoped that *The Pickwick Papers* might please you.'

'Thank you!' Bytheway settled to listen as the maid began to read. He was fond of the book, and when the maid read one of the funniest passages he could barely refrain from laughing.

'Don't move!' came the sharp command.

Deacon began to polish the plate with silk, rubbing furiously. As he polished it, it lost its silver colour and became black. Next he focused the lens upon Bytheway. 'Keep on,' he said, as the maid flagged slightly. 'Keep still, George,' he repeated.

Deacon had worked so hard at the polishing that his round-ended nose gleamed and the apples shone in his cheeks. Of a sudden, he disappeared under a tent which occupied one corner of the room. Under the tent he made the plate sensitive to light, passing it through the coating boxes, which were so pungent. The maid, meanwhile, continued reading.

After some seconds, Deacon emerged, brandishing the plate. Quick as a flash he took it from its cover and put it into the camera. 'Keep still!'

With his watch in his hand, Deacon counted out two minutes. He was now like a kettle that boiled over. Waiting infuriated him, and so he dissipated his energy by shifting leg to leg. Was the watch broken? He wanted to shake his timepiece, but suddenly he removed the plate and put it over a heated bath, which was peculiar, like a downturned pyramid. Deacon waited for fine mercury beads to form on the plate, then doused it in a solution of hyposulphate of soda and washed it in gold chloride. All that remained was for Deacon to wash the plate, dry it and insert it into a frame behind glass. Thereafter, Deacon took the picture to Bytheway, but hardly allowed him to look at it.

'Another,' he said.

'May I see it, please?'

'No.'

'One moment, please!' Bytheway had expected there to be a period of recuperation. He wanted some fresh air and to stretch his legs. Deacon, however, meant to proceed, and to dispense with their reader, too.

'Thank you, Miss Brawn.'

Bytheway had been enjoying the book, but without consultation it was withdrawn. Ignoring him, Deacon began to polish another plate, but Bytheway began to feel the discomfort of the clamps behind his ears.

'Might I be released, Mr Deacon?'

'No.'

Bytheway blew out his cheeks. This had not been the answer that he had expected. The smell alone might have initiated a break, but Deacon did not seem to notice and kept on polishing.

'You are such a backward fellow,' said Deacon suddenly. The sweat glistened on his forehead. 'You and your damned superstitions. Surely this process, if anything, should make you believe in science? Progress, George, progress.'

Bytheway began to breathe heavily.

'Stop that,' said Deacon. He was now rubbing the plate with his silk wad. 'This is a miracle, to catch a moment as it passes! Never mind your Good Book: here is a miracle taking place before your eyes.'

'Have you trapped me within this chair, sir, so that you may torment me?' demanded Bytheway. His pleasant, handsome face was clouded: brows down, cheeks bunched, eyes disagreeable.

'I do not mean to torment you, only encourage you to think. Reason, George, reason.'

Deacon disappeared under the tent again. Under the tent he exposed the plate, alternately, to bromide, iodine and chloride. Once again, with the plate primed, he protected it in a case and emerged into the daylight. With a flourish he inserted it into the camera, removing the protective cover before he did so.

'Keep still!' Once more, with the cover off the camera lens, Deacon began counting the two minutes. 'Do not move. Do not say anything. Keep still.' All the time he looked at his watch, rather like a railway stationmaster. 'Might you make an idol of me since I have performed this miracle before you? No. You see, there are no makers of miracles and never were, except those that you see now, and their god is Science.'

Throughout the two minutes Deacon alternated between telling Bytheway to be still and insulting his faith. Like an animal caught in a gamekeeper's trap and exhausted from struggling, Bytheway sat still, said nothing, did nothing but waited to be released. When the two minutes had elapsed Deacon ignored him, so that Bytheway set to struggling with the clips behind his ears. Deacon looked up briefly just once.

The clamps behind his head were awkward to release. In his efforts to free himself Bytheway even lost a little hair.

'One moment,' said Deacon, who bent over the image. As before his face shone with sweat. 'One moment.'

Finally Deacon finished, and released Bytheway. As he did so he pulled a reproving face. 'There was no occasion for panic.'

Bytheway, poisoned by fumes, was sweaty too; there were the makings of dark patches under his arms. He looked at Deacon once, then kept his eyes to himself. Deacon returned his glance, as if he could barely remain patient with him, his expression suggesting that he thought Bytheway was like a backward child who was much to be pitied. Was it really appropriate for a grown man to make such a fuss? Surely not!

Bytheway gathered his thoughts.

'Another?' said Deacon.

'No,' said Bytheway. 'No, thank you.'

The two men looked at each other.

'Your image,' said Deacon. 'I need it. When I have finished with it you may have it.'

It had been Bytheway's understanding that he would leave with his image. Somehow he felt cheated. It seemed, however, that his employer had finished with him. Deacon did not say anything, but began upon something else, almost as if he had forgotten him. Of course, Bytheway had no choice but to remember his station; in consequence of this he bowed. He bowed, however, without response. He said a few courteous words, too, to the back of Deacon's head. Deacon half acknowledged them; he lifted a hand, or some such. For a rather long moment Bytheway looked at the back of Deacon's head. Clearly he considered his employer. In truth, he despised his own civility towards this man who, even now, had his back turned to him, yet something kept him hoping for the merest pleasantry or approbation. Like a dog, Bytheway lingered for some recognition, some word of civility in return for his own.

'You may go,' said Deacon. This was an end to it; this was his release. Even now Deacon did not look at him. Bytheway was left to find his own way out, although one of the servants remembered her manners and showed him to the door. Such was his exit. He was annoyed as he had expected to leave with his image, but all the same he was free. Oh, to be out of the smell of chemicals, out into the clean air! About were all the colours of the many-coloured day, and movement and life going on. The sun was bright and the cathedral was like a flower opening. It was like a fairytale castle, as beautiful as could be. The city about him, too, was all roofs and chimneys, all huddle and windows winking. Bytheway fairly clattered down the drive and escaped. At the back of his mind he wondered why Deacon had retained his image, but for the moment just to escape was enough.

Chapter Seven

Word circulated in Lichfield that the next meeting of the Philosophical Club would be especially interesting. The evening was likely to be 'instructive', 'one of the best in recent memory'. One might also have added the word 'controversial': Deacon was to be their speaker, and no one had forgotten his objection to Bytheway's ghost story. If all else failed there might at least be an argument.

Bytheway might easily have avoided the meeting but would not do so. Perhaps he saw himself as a champion, obliged to defend the Faith, as though the Church had tied her handkerchief to his lance. So he was patient towards all the people asking him to attend the event, such as Woodhouse, who begged his colleague to go. In fact, so many men begged him to go that Bytheway felt compelled to attend, despite his reservations.

As the days went past the meeting seemed to become a beacon: a sense of occasion developed about it, the press reported it and so on, so that Lichfield counted the days until the event. When one day follows another, everything comes, and so it was with the talk. On the appointed night the members arrived pink and scrubbed, although it was kind not to inspect what they wore. It was common for men to wear clothes which were patched, but they came to drink of the knowledge which might improve them and better their station.

Of course, there was a limit to the difference which occasional lectures could make to these men, but the members remained aspirational, and it was poignant that the building had the look of a college. There was a spire, too, rising over them, not the dreaming spires of Oxford but a spire, which lent something to the scene. St Mary's Church stood just behind the Corn Exchange and demanded notice with its bizarre combination of styles. It seemed odd on a first viewing: the body of the church remained Classical, while the spire was Gothic.

The members scurried along. As if a bell were tolling from its roof, the building seemed to draw people. How exciting, too, to step out of the night and into the light. Inside the hall was the energy of a hundred men assembled with common purpose. The stir in that room compared with that of a factory: there was bustle and noise, chairs scraping, people moving, men laughing, friends seeking one another out and, like an offering, blue tobacco smoke swirling in the lights. Centre stage, like an priest, stood Deacon.

Under observation, Deacon took out his gold watch and cleaned it. The light reflected from it and he wanted people to notice it; however, perhaps he expended some nervous energy. He may have been feeling a little jumpy. As he waited, he rubbed his hands, cleared his throat and occasionally fidgeted. Sometimes he turned round to check his equipment. Behind him were a series of easels, each covered, and two chairs, one for Deacon and one for Mr Rowbotham. Eventually Rowbotham decided that they should start. By the authority vested in him as chairman he took up a bell and tinkled it.

'Em-em-em-em, gentlemen, if you please?' The bell tinkled again. 'Gentlemen, please. Gentlemen.' Tinkle, tinkle. 'Gentlemen'.

The last mouths gradually stopped working. Finally the very last jaws were operating and their owners felt embarrassed.

These people glanced round with a look which seemed to suggest, 'Can you possibly be waiting for me?' So the room at last became quiet. Next came a moment or two of fidgeting. The company settled down and, at last, looked forward. Deacon regarded them. He noticed how people seemed to sit where they always sat. He could find people where he knew they would be, and so he found Bytheway and Woodhouse. Bytheway looked good natured but shuffled; he rubbed his hands too, and licked his lips. Woodhouse was Woodhouse. With his long chin and high hairline, his slightly off -centre face, his high cheekbones and narrow eyes he looked sly, as if he expected something. He and Deacon exchanged a glance.

'Gentlemen, gentlemen,' began Mr Rowbotham. He stood to his full height and his jaw wagged, as if it were loose at its pivots. He crouched now, turned from side to side and looked into the rafters. 'Gentlemen. We, em-em-em, are gathered here for a talk from our esteemed member Mr Deacon. I'm sure that we shall find it most instructive. Mr Deacon wants, em-em-em, to make some observations about the expression of emotions in animals and draw some conclusions regarding our own capacity to communicate in a non-verbal manner. I'm sure that he will delight us all. Mr Deacon.'

Rowbotham raised his hands to applaud and so did the audience. Deacon stood with his chin down, but accepted the applause as his due.

'Gentlemen,' he said at last, raising his head. 'You may know that I've had an ape in my care for some weeks now. I'm soon to return the animal to her keeper and have been at some pains to study the creature. In these drawings,' Deacon's voice took on a greater emphasis, 'I have captured various expressions upon the face of the animal which correspond to different emotions.' He swept the cover from the nearest easel. 'You will, of course, forgive the poor quality of my sketches.'

Deacon left a space for contradiction. There was a moment of hiatus, then someone spoke up. 'Not at all, Mr Deacon.'

Silence, then someone else took the cue. 'Excellent, excellent, Mr Deacon.'

'Bravo,' said somebody else.

'Indeed they're excellent,' said Mr Rowbotham. He stood up and raised his hands again, and dutifully there was a round of applause.

Deacon smiled and bowed. 'They're but trifles, trifles, gentlemen. You're most kind.' He raised a hand in a kind of benediction. 'Thank you! Thank you, one and all. Now, gentlemen, consider: here we see the ape in a state of concentration. The animal, for her amusement, was attempting to crush flies against the windows in her enclosure. The flies were difficult to pin down, and so we may observe her complete absorption. Gentlemen, observe your wives when they are sewing. Note how they press their lips together in concentration as they thread a needle. Note, too, that the lips of the animal are somewhat extended. Is this not a trait we see in ourselves? Gentlemen, is it not curious that we and the animal share these characteristics?'

Deacon pulled the covers from two more easels. On each was a drawing of an ape or monkey, expertly done. Deacon had commissioned an artist to produce the drawings and had spared no expense. The first showed a chimpanzee, which was unwell and in a state of abject self pity. Deacon pointed to its listless appearance. 'I'm not fortunate enough to have a child, but those of you who are fathers may surely recognise such a condition in your children when they have been unwell: the listlessness, dull eyes and dropped countenance. Indeed, I understand that young chimpanzees, in violent passion, may present a strong resemblance to children in a similar state. I have a report of a chimpanzee, enraged at having some favourite food denied her, who rolled about, throwing her arms out, screaming with a widely opened mouth and biting everything within her reach. Here again, gentleman, we find the expressions of an animal being closely analogous to those of Man.'

Deacon went on to describe the next image, which represented a monkey in a state of distress. The picture was curious; as Deacon admitted, there was some licence in its composition. None the less, the fact of the case was compelling: that a monkey was capable of crying. He reported the testimony of two zookeepers, who attested to seeing this expression of emotion, and again drew parallels with human behaviour.

Two rows back in the audience, Bytheway began to shift in his seat and, as he moved, Woodhouse glanced at him. Bytheway had grown red, although he continued to try and 'behave'; that is, he sat with his back straight, showing polite interest. As ever, his eyes gave him away. He had fine eyes, which were lit and expressive, and Woodhouse seemed to read them well.

'I don't think Mr Deacon should do this, Mr B. We see the purpose of this; that Man is an ape and no more. He's not showing our faith any respect, in my opinion. I don't like it myself, sir, I'm sure I don't. What are you going to do about it? Are you going to say something? I dare not say anything, not in my position, but a senior clerk like you, sir, deserves more respect.'

Deacon seemed to hear Woodhouse chattering and glanced up. When Woodhouse stopped talking Deacon immediately returned to his business, and Woodhouse looked back at Bytheway, catching his eye. He jabbed a discreet finger at Deacon and made a gesture that seemed to indicate outrage.

Deacon concluded his remarks about monkeys that cried, then drew back the covers upon two more easels. The gentlemen were presented with two drawings, one of an orang-utan looking rather humorous and a second in which the same animal looked less good natured.

'In this first image, gentlemen, we see the orang in my keeping after she'd been tickled. The animal, again like a human child, is particularly susceptible to tickling, especially under the armpits, which produces a decided chuckling noise. If this operation is momentarily suspended the corners of the animal's mouth are drawn back, which produces a grin. This drawing back of the lips may also be accompanied by wrinkling of the skin at the edge of the eyes. Observe, too, if you please, how the eyes have grown brighter. Are not the characteristics that I've described fully indicative of our own laughter? The second image, gentlemen.' Deacon glanced again at Bytheway. 'Observe, if you will, this image of my orang enraged by having an orange offered and then denied her. You will note how the animal has protruded her lips. The animal produces a similar expression when alarmed, but this protrusion of the lips is particularly associated with disappointment, sulkiness and irritation. A similar pouting of the lips may sometimes be seen in children and, indeed, in some adults. Now, gentlemen.'

Deacon danced like a pixie to a further two easels, rubbing his hands. 'I've been able to augment my lecture this evening by use of two daguerreotype images.'

Two rows away Bytheway coloured and shook his head, just once. He closed his eyes briefly and did not notice Woodhouse, nodding again and pointing toward the front, trying to engage his attention.

'Here, gentlemen.'

The covers were withdrawn with a great flourish, and the company was presented with two pictures of Mr Bytheway. At once a sort of cry went up. There was a mixed reaction to the images; some men were shocked, but many laughed as Bytheway found himself the butt of one or two jokes. Only men on a equal social footing indulged in jests, of course, but what pricked Bytheway was the fact that his inferiors, working men, shared in the laughter.

'You will see,' said Deacon, 'with my apologies, of course, to Mr Bytheway, that he exhibits the same characteristics as the ape. In this image we see a smile on the lips of Mr Bytheway. His eyes, too, are amused.'

Deacon pointed to a very pleasing image of Bytheway, in which he smiled at the reading from *The Pickwick Papers*. Bytheway looked every inch what he was: good natured; his eyes were warm and his lips had a discernible smile upon them, which turned the corners of his mouth.

'Mr Bytheway was amused by a rendition of a comic novel, gentlemen. Notice the drawing back of the lips, the wrinkling at the eyes and their brightness; is not this, essentially, the same animal as the ape? Now we turn to the other image.'

'I'm afraid that Mr Deacon is making a monkey out of you, Mr B.,' said Woodhouse. 'Are you going to let him do it and say nothing? Are you, sir?'

Bytheway did not know how to respond. He sat silently with his hands bunching in his lap, but glanced around.

'In this second image we see Mr Bytheway provoked. You will recall, gentlemen, that the orang protruded her lips when angry. Notice how Mr Bytheway, in this image, has pursed his lips and protruded them, although, I admit, not to the same degree as the ape. Observe, I believe he might be doing something similar now.'

All at once the company turned to Bytheway; from left and right they turned; behind him they craned their necks to see; the front row turned round; neighbours on his row intruded upon him; Deacon stared. Rowbotham peered, his jaw wagging. It was too much.

'Mr Deacon, I protest,' shouted Bytheway. He jumped to his feet. 'How can you insult me in this way and invite people to ridicule me? How can you suggest that I am no more than an animal?'

'But that is it, George,' said Deacon calmly. 'We're all no more than that. There is no cause for anger, sir. You forget yourself, Mr Bytheway.'

The evening hung suspended; no one said anything. Bytheway stood and Deacon stared at him.

'Shall we ask the company, Mr Deacon, if anyone else finds this talk objectionable? I see gentlemen here whom I know attend worship regularly. Indeed, most of us attend church every Sunday. Do you realise, gentlemen, the import of Mr Deacon's lecture? He'd have us be beasts; a better sort of beast, perhaps, but no more than that. What do you say, gentlemen, are we not more than that?'

A chair scraped here and there and several men got up, and save for the noise of their boots on the wooden floor they silently left the room. Among the remainder some had their faces down and many arms were folded, and a shuffling began. Some of them wanted Deacon to continue, however; some wanted more entertainment.

'Gentlemen,' said Rowbotham. 'Em-em-em.'

'Does she have a soul, Mr Deacon?' said Bytheway. 'Yes, the ape may be made from the same clay, but has not the Almighty given us a soul?'

'Are we back again to that, George? The gentlemen must believe what they please but I tell you there is no soul. There is no survival of the spirit! We are animals, and you and your kind have codded us long enough. You and your Holy Revelation ... has science taught you nothing? You must confront the truth of it, George, like it or not.'

'I do not like it, sir,' said Bytheway, 'and I don't agree with you.' He sat down.

For a moment Deacon said nothing, but he looked at Bytheway, half in disgust and half with a sort of pity which might ordinarily have been reserved for unwanted kittens before they were drowned.

'How I despise you in your superstition,' he said at last. May I suggest that you whistle to yourself on the way home tonight if you are frightened in the dark, and perhaps leave the candle burning when you pull the bed covers over your head?'

Bytheway sat and fought his impulse to storm out. Many eyes settled on him again. Men who were normally deferential stared at him; men of a lower standing laughed at his expense or discussed him within his hearing, and Bytheway, against every wish, felt himself flush, until he knew that his face was burning. Once again, some of the company elbowed one another and pointed out his embarrassment, too.

'If you've quite finished, Mr Bytheway?' said Deacon. He tossed his head and strutted about, sticking out his chest.

'I wouldn't stand for it, Mr B.,' muttered Woodhouse. 'I wouldn't stand for it.'

And so the meeting went on.

Chapter Eight

One Sunday, when the bells were ringing, Bytheway sat beside Carney, who was propped up in bed. Carney was bilious, but Bytheway collected this liquid in a pot, unembarrassed and stoic. Sometimes he soiled his hands in helping Carney, although it was in being there that he did most good. The friends sat in an awareness of each other, although occasionally in silence.

'Not fair, not fair,' said Carney, suddenly.

'What, my friend?'

'The daguerreotypes.' He tried to say more, but a pulse passed over him. This pulse was followed by a retch, and as Bytheway stood poised with the pot the fluid found a blockage. Suddenly the bile gathered. Carney could neither expel it, nor swallow it, until it mounted in him and blocked his airways. He would have drowned there and then, but Bytheway, without fuss, rubbed his back until the phlegm drooled out.

There was something routine in Bytheway doing this, something practised, and whatever he did he did with the least embarrassment or intrusion. When Carney began to struggle again, Bytheway primed him like a seasoned nurse. Once primed, like a pump that coughs and sputters, Carney expelled the muck without help from anyone else.

All this went beyond the expectations of friendship, and it was good of Bytheway to be so giving because he did not enjoy it. His face was telling as he wiped his fingers. That said, he felt ashamed when distaste for Carney's plight entered his thoughts or he had to force himself to visit his friend. His one consolation was that he was welcome there. The people who were left to Carney, of whom he was one, were those Carney wanted.

Among the people whom Carney wanted his housekeeper brought him most comfort. She excelled in what was attainable by touch and a soft word. Today she was at church, and in her absence Bytheway surprised himself. When Carney was suddenly seized by pain, neither sitting up, lying down nor rubbing relieved it, and he sobbed. In that moment something happened that Bytheway did not expect. He jumped up and cupped his right hand around the face of his friend, soothing him; and Carney ceased crying. For Bytheway it was a moment of revelation. He even looked at his hand, which had brought such comfort. Thereafter, Bytheway freely took his friend's hand. This was hardly the thing between male friends, not at all, but he did it and Carney held him tight, rocking slightly as he did so, rocking and sighing; and so the time went on.

Once, after an interval of silence, Carney spoke. 'George, I am frightened.'

Bytheway's chair creaked. His answer, such as it was, was to squeeze his friend's hand.

'There is no escape,' said Carney. 'Where shall I hide? You would think that I should be glad to die, but I am frightened. Dear Lord, may I die when I am asleep. I hope that I may die when I am asleep.'

Suddenly emotion squeezed out of Bytheway. It forced its way up his gut, stormed up his throat, filled his eyes. This would never do! Men should not cry. He pushed any thought of weeping from his mind and considered some nonsense; at the same time he attempted to regulate his breathing. For a moment his deep inhalations kept pace with those of Carney.

'Pray with me,' said Carney. 'Pray with me, won't you, George?'

And so it was that Bytheway came to a moment of crisis. He did not know what to say. For a moment the truth almost spilled from him. He felt he had to confess, to himself as much as Carney, that his faith had withered, that he no longer knew whether he believed or not. In that moment he wanted to rage against Deacon and the scientific cabal, and protest to his God that Carney should be dying as he was, so unjustly, and in so much pain.

'I imagine, my friend,' said Bytheway, despite everything, 'that dying is like the passing from one room to another. A doorway, that is all.'

'Yes,' said Carney, catching hold of the thought. 'Yes.'

They were silent again, remaining as they were for a minute or more.

'George,' said Carney again. 'You will pray for me, will you not?'

Bytheway said something encouraging.

'George.'

'What?'

'Has your faith left you, even you?'

'No,' said Bytheway. 'No. At least not entirely. Not entirely.'

'Even you,' said Carney.

Carney, as if his hands were suspended from strings, covered his eyes. Bytheway shifted on his chair and begged Carney to look at him. Carney removed his hands but kept his eyes closed. 'Charles,' said Bytheway. 'Charles.' The enormity of his confession suddenly appalled Bytheway.

'May the good Lord help me!' He put his hands up to his face and brought them down again, half got up, sat down, and did not know what to do or say. 'On every side my faith is assaulted! Darwin: the inescapable logic of *The Origin*, Lyell showing the great age of the earth, Huxley, fossils showing that animals were

49

not made once and once only, Deacon rubbing my nose in it all, and such human misery. You, my friend, what have you done to find yourself there?' Once more tears forced themselves up Bytheway's throat. He took a great shuddering gasp but he was choked, just briefly. He did not know where to put himself, and Carney took his hand. 'No!' said Bytheway, 'I shall not cry! Such a spectacle. Forgive me, Charles.' He snatched his hand away and rocked like a nursery toy.

'Do not cry, George,' said Carney, softly. 'Do not distress yourself. I will not pretend,' he said, gathering his breath, 'that there are not times when my faith seems feeble and even the name of Christ seems no more than a name. Sometimes I lie here and fear the dark. At such times I am miserable, I do not deny it, but in the end my faith will uphold me, I know it!'

Bytheway could not say anything at first. 'You comfort me, Charles,' he said at last, aware of the irony. 'You comfort me!'

Carney seemed pleased at this. He smiled and gave a little nod. His smile glowed like cinders in the morning, but the friends shared a moment of concord. The two men were pleased with each other. Bytheway settled in his seat again, and looked on as his friend lay back for a minute's peace. Carney wanted to close his eyes for just a moment, but was soon asleep. As he slept, his chest rose and fell, up and down, as if he had not a care in the world.

So it was that Bytheway left his friend, by and by. Although Carney could not hear him, Bytheway promised to come again tomorrow, although he hoped that Carney might die in his sleep before then. Bytheway, chief clerk, gentleman, raised his own hands to his own tired-looking face and covered his eyes. He wore all the garb of a gentleman: coat, shawl-collared waistcoat and crisp white shirt, cravat and braces, checked wool trousers and had a top hat beside the bed, but felt like a child. It was true that Carney had comforted him, but it was a threadbare comfort, and Bytheway felt something mounting in him. He suddenly felt unequal to everything. He could not bear this godlessness, nor the sceptics and the empiricists, nor the carping of Deacon. He felt a sort of rage toward Deacon, in truth. He clamped a hand to his mouth and looked round him, noticing a large pair of scissors on the cupboard near the bed. He looked at these as a dog would at a rabbit. Suddenly Bytheway was on his feet and dropping down the stairs two steps at a time. He was going somewhere in a hurry, although he could not say exactly where.

A few short minutes afterwards Bytheway found himself at his destination. It was as if he had been led there. To think of it, all the time his mind had been working and now his purpose became clear. Bytheway had arrived on the platform of the railway station. There was a train due shortly, and he now realised that he had some business with it. Ludicrously, someone approached him and so a pantomime took place. Mr Bytheway acted out interest but it was completely bogus. He concealed his distraction, but someone who knew him well might have noticed it. More than being disinterested, Bytheway was odd, too: he laughed too loudly, for example, and gabbled. His strangeness went unnoticed, however; but a more observant person would have noted it and remembered it at the inquest, because Bytheway meant to throw himself under a train.

The departure of the chatterbox was one of the sweetest moments in Bytheway's life. He might even have been rude had someone else bothered him. Thankfully no one troubled him and he began to think. What would people say, he wondered, when he was dead? 'Who would have thought it?' 'Poor old George.' No doubt the inquest would discuss the balance of his mind. The coroner might do as he pleased. Bytheway's one recurring thought about the inquest was of the embarrassment which would be caused to Deacon. He hoped that Deacon would be sorry; but to the business at hand.

It seemed to Bytheway that timing was everything. If he jumped too soon he might have time to change his mind. Someone else might try to save him, and they could be killed. No, let him time it right. If anyone distracted him he might mistime his jump, so he pretended preoccupation with a timetable, as if he were planning a journey. The irony struck him that he was doing exactly this, although his destination did not appear on the printed sheet.

There was a tremble in Bytheway now, working up his legs – but it was not fear. He was like a dog in the traps. He glanced down the track: nothing yet, but the train would not be long. Once again he had to contain himself, and sought distraction. The station became the sole focus of his attention. It was, he told himself, a handsome building in respectful style. Respectful style, he repeated. Respectful style. He fixed his mind upon it. It presented two bays, each crowned by a gable. Between each bay was a row of columns and the whole structure, with some attendant buildings along it, extended some way along the track. Quoins decorated its leading edges, and it was altogether handsome. There were echoes of an earlier England in its design; perhaps its nostalgia softened the shock of the new? Change was often galling to people who wanted to cling to what they knew.

The track stretched off to his right, and away beyond the bridge, under which the train would come, St Michael's Church stood abreast its hill, trees round it, a symbol of a different age. It stood on an ancient, holy site and represented a time of old truths, before the world changed, before the ground shifted under his feet.

Bytheway looked at the headstones round the church. He almost envied the dead. They had lived and died in the old certainties, certainties that were denied to him. He had been marked out by time to have his faith eroded. How could an intelligent man who read not be confronted by 'facts' too awful to tell? Science seemed to have undone the old order. Even the consolation of natural theology proposed by Paley, which suggested design in everything by a benevolent creator, was overset. Darwin had shown that life was nothing but a struggle for existence, and life forms better suited by chance to prosper would do so at the expense of those less favoured. Benign nature was a myth.

At that moment as he stood by the track, watching a train approach, it seemed to Bytheway correct that he should throw himself under its wheels. If he were to time his action rightly he would not suffer; there would be a moment, no more, of agony, and then it would be done.

The train came nearer, still very new, friendly looking. It had a chimney like a stovepipe hat, which produced puff-puff-puffs of smoke. Behind it snaked the carriages. People were already gathering on the platform, and a child on the sidings jumped up and down. The boy was excited; the train did not bring his death.

It seemed to Bytheway that there was nothing left. His respectable career, his £400 a year, his good name, everything, seemed worthless. The loss of his faith made everything desolate. Materialism offered only the here and now, one sensation followed by another, whereas he had enjoyed a prospect of eternity. He had believed himself, and those he loved, to be leaves on a stream that would carry them all away. There had been a great ocean in his mind that would receive them all. To put it another way, whether he lived or died he was at one with God; he existed in a continuum, and nothing could ever separate him from the Almighty, from love and hope and permanence in an impermanent world. This faith had underpinned almost every thought; it had sustained him and nourished him; and now it had been snatched from him.

Bytheway could blame Huxley and Lyell and Darwin, of course, among others, but there was one man whom he blamed above all: his employer, Deacon. He could not forgive his malice; he could not forgive him for seeking to rob him of his faith.

He watched the train. It pulled up, hissing steam, screeching. There was a moment just before the motion ran out of it that he thought of jumping, but another idea had occurred to George Bytheway. It might be that he would have his moment of consummation with the train another time, but not now. He turned on his heels and strode off; he could hardly wait for the opening of the bank the next day. He, chief clerk, long-time, trusted employee, Mr Sensible, Mr Honest, Mr Christian, would steal from the bank.

Chapter Nine

The next morning, before it was properly light, Bytheway slipped into the bank. He took refuge in his familiar seat and sat with his head in his hands, thinking. He remained almost motionless, then got up and removed the cancelled notes from the safe. He looked at the money and popped it inside his pocket: there, he had stolen it. He took the notes out again and became a bank clerk; he put them in his pocket and became a thief. Finally he got up and returned the bundle to the safe.

Bytheway returned to his desk as if lacking sufficient strength to cross the floor, but soon got up to look for Woodhouse. As usual, Woodhouse arrived just in time. How Bytheway disliked him! His Christian self made him guilty but, he supposed, he was free to dislike Woodhouse now. Woodhouse settled behind his high wooden desk, hot after his rush to work, and Bytheway watched him. Woodhouse's long face (made longer by his hair, which was already retreating) was flushed. His high cheekbones, his slanting, crooked mouth, his narrow eyes made him look secretive. He certainly looked like an accomplice, Bytheway thought; he would not need corrupting.

Bytheway continued to watch Woodhouse and Woodhouse, though he had his head down, seemed to sense it. The tension grew between them. The clock beat time and they listened to it, although ordinarily they did not know it was there. The words sometimes formed in Bytheway's throat, the words that would make him a thief. These words were like a fish bone. In trying to speak he had to master himself, but he kept on trying to cough them up.

Woodhouse glanced at him, beginning to take an interest, but then unexpectedly Deacon arrived. Up they got, chairs scraping. The two men bowed, although Deacon paid them no particular notice. None the less, he brought a cold wind in with him. The tension in the bank somehow increased, the more so as no one said anything.

That morning customers kept them busy. There were civilities to exchange; proprieties. The everyday business of the day had to take its course, but somehow there was a sense of something extraordinary between them. Perhaps for that reason Deacon sometimes came into their space, as if to sniff the air, although he said little. Bytheway glanced at Woodhouse and Woodhouse glanced at him.

Bytheway realised that he was waiting for Deacon to leave. Even as he talked with Deacon, too, Bytheway contemplated stealing from the bank. There was time to reconsider but, somehow, this thing was already in motion.

Some time later, after lingering for some reason as though he were reluctant to leave, Deacon went. He said that he was going home; nothing more, not even a goodbye. The door closed heavily behind him, the doorbell jangled and then became still. Woodhouse raised his long, crooked face. Bytheway got up, went to the safe, removed the package of notes and put half of them on the desk in front of Woodhouse.

'I'll join you in your scheme to steal from the bank,' he said.

Woodhouse turned white, then a pink tinge crept over him. All the time he stared at the money, looking like a mouse eyeing the cheese in a trap.

'I've grown tired of Mr Deacon,' said Bytheway. He swallowed hard. 'And I mean to punish him.'

Woodhouse measured him. The clock tick-tocked, tick-tocked, tick-tocked.

'Well, Mr Woodhouse?'

Woodhouse twisted his lips and thought, his narrow eyes growing narrower. Finally his lust for money overcame him. 'I mean to be in Canada or Australia before they come for me,' he said suddenly. In that moment he was all excitement and jumped up like a monkey, twice at least, from his seat. 'What about you?'

'Don't concern yourself with me,' said Bytheway.

For a moment the conspirators looked at each another. Bytheway, chief clerk, was smart and respectable as ever, but stared at the key which had made him a criminal and the stuffing had gone from him. Woodhouse, for his part, sat up like a child on Christmas morning. His eyes glittered, and as he watched his colleague a smile spread from ear to ear.

'I thought I'd have to tell you how to do it, George,' he rattled. 'Do you know it occurred to me some while ago? You sign the bank notes, you issue them and you withdraw them. Why shouldn't we keep the notes that are meant to be decommissioned? Am I not a clever fellow?'

'It's simple enough.'

It was indeed simple enough. The bank issued its own notes, under guarantee of the London bank Goodfellow, James and Fiddick. Bytheway signed each note, and whenever one was issued he recorded its number in a ledger. Conversely, when a note was withdrawn he cancelled it by removing the number, and logged the nullification of that note in a register. The notes were retained by the bank for inspection and now, largely forgotten, had amassed into a considerable sum.

It seemed to Woodhouse that they might make lots and lots of money. He rubbed his hands and contemplated the riches that they would accrue. For some minutes he could think of nothing else. As in a trance, he ran his thumb along the wad of notes: so much for clothes, so much for a watch, so much for travel to

London: theatres, wine and women. A smile spread over his face and he looked at Bytheway, pitying him but not with malice.

'I'll introduce you to some ladies, George. They'll like to meet you now that you're a moneyed gentleman; not that they'd have given tuppence for you before, I daresay. We'll have you pop that cork of yours yet, eh?'

Bytheway winced. 'We must be careful,' he said, his thin lips pressed into a line. 'We must not be seen to come into money suddenly. We must be prudent.'

'Prudent!' Woodhouse laughed.

'Prudent,' said Bytheway.

'Ever the bank clerk, eh, George? I'll consider the matter,' said Woodhouse, doing a fair impression of imitating Deacon. 'But don't forget that we're equal partners now: no more of this chief clerk nonsense if you please! I tell you, I am too slippery a fish for old Deacon to catch me.'

So it was that the matter was sealed between them. There could be no turning back. Woodhouse went home whistling, his cheeks like harvest-time apples. Even to the last, however, Bytheway wanted to call him back and tell him, beg him, bribe him to return the money, but quickly Woodhouse was beyond his reach.

Of course, it was purely by chance but that night a storm raged over Lichfield. Bytheway lay in bed and listened to the rain drumming outside. Unable to sleep, he stood in the window and watched as a lightning bolt struck the cathedral. It was a wild, superstitious thought, but he wondered if he threw the stolen notes from the window whether the storm would cease. It was a silly thought, but in the morning there was another circumstance which rocked him: people walking near Deacon's house, where the path wandered beside the pool, found a tree cleaved down the middle. Seemingly, if the chatter was believed, it had been an unprecedented night in Lichfield. One might have thought that the world had shifted sideways or the natural order was overset. Bytheway tried to be patient with such talk, but he was uncomfortable with it for all that; and meanwhile the stolen notes burned like cinders in his wallet.

Chapter Ten

Deacon looked from the west-facing drawing room in his house. Over Stowe Pool the cathedral rose up and the greater spire was framed by the smaller ones. He tried to see it as his wife had: Mrs Deacon, full of Tennyson's poems, had likened it to Camelot. Deacon was unable to picture the knights riding two by two toward it, nor could he say exactly when his wife had died, but she was gone; that was the crux of it: gone. Yet how could she be gone? Even now he caught himself looking round for her.

In the window, with his snub nose and ruff of whiskers, he looked like a cat watching, waiting for someone to come home, although in fact he studied his reflection. He thought how strange it was that he could be so rich, but so miserable. That day he had told the children of the workhouse how industry and honesty would make them happy, which he believed; although he doubted it for himself. At least if they had money they might find some comfort in life. It seemed to him that there was nothing else. He had been robbed of those he cared for, and what was left, save his work and the consolation and distraction of material possessions: his house, the farm, his carriages, watches, paintings and money?

It was these things that marked him out from those wretches in the workhouse. Thus, if unhappiness ever threatened him he bought something. The house was full of these things, the best this, the latest that, and he kept a close eye on all his neighbours. When one friend seemed likely to outdo him, Deacon had broken off their friendship.

This materialism was only part of the man, however. He was also a guardian of the workhouse and, *ipso facto*, of its children. Even when absent from it, Deacon knew the business of the workhouse, and its staff knew that he would not condone abuse of the children. Just as Deacon had appointed them so might he dismiss them, and they remembered that. He even displayed towards the children a sort of bluff kindness.

In addition, Deacon also campaigned for children. Despite his busy life he read reports concerning working children. These accounts paraphrased the submissions of child workers: guileless testimonies of hard lives from children who knew nothing else. Deacon wanted the law changed to protect children, and corresponded with people who shared his interest. One such was a clergyman who was connected to Lord Shaftsbury, the great champion of working children: so it was, by one remove, that Deacon exerted his influence in the highest reaches of government. However, Deacon and his clergyman friend did not agree upon everything; for example, religious education divided them. Deacon disliked religious study *per se,* but Church and Sunday Schools often provided the only tuition a child received. So it was that Deacon lobbied for children to be educated by the state.

It was strange, but perhaps typical, that Deacon had investments in factories employing young children. This contradiction did not seem to occur to him. In regard to adults he was entirely consistent, however. He believed that people prospered according to the choices they made. Moreover, he believed 'bad luck' to be a fig leaf for loafers. There was no misfortune, he thought, that a man might not overcome. If people failed in life it was because of vice and the giving way to temptation. In short, people received their due, and his own outstanding position was no more than a reflection of his worth. Similarly, the spreading of Britain's empire across the globe seemed to Deacon a reflection of the technological and moral superiority of the British race. Britons were triumphant because they deserved to be so: indeed, they were the true heirs to Creation, managing the affairs of other nations that were less able to do so for themselves.

In his good works – and there were many – Deacon compensated for the loss of his wife and children. If some good came of their deaths then their lives had not been in vain. He was so busy that he neglected the bank, but Old George was a reliable old stick and ran it for him while his attention was elsewhere.

Deacon felt momentarily sorry about Bytheway. He knew that he had treated him badly. To tell the truth, he had decided not to torment his chief clerk any longer, partly frightened that Bytheway might leave to join a rival bank, and partly having realised that he deserved better, being well-meaning and loyal. However, as he considered Bytheway the thought was crushed by the recollection of his family, and he became just as miserable as before. There was something about their deaths that he could not admit to himself. Once again, the demon accosted him, came upon him, and he wrestled with it and forced it from his mind. Leaning heavily on the sill, as if he were trying to keep the terrible truth inside its box, he closed his eyes until the moment passed. Just as he thought it was mastered it burst out again. Once more he had to face it, think of it, something he would not have done willingly for the world.

The terrible truth was that he had killed his wife, and his children; he had killed them all.

Chapter Eleven

Bytheway made his way up Beacon Street, en route to visit Woodhouse. His way took him past the cathedral and Bytheway was tempted to look. The cathedral was dear to him, but he turned away and looked at a house instead. The grandfather of Charles Darwin had lived in that house, though, so he turned from it too.

That day was Sunday and it was unusual for the two clerks to socialise with each other. Another thing was unusual, too: Bytheway was going to meet a woman. Mr Bytheway was to drink tea with Woodhouse and two ladies. For some reason, Bytheway felt wicked and so – poor man – the more he felt it necessary to walk his 'respectable' walk. None the less, he wore fashionable clothes, glossy shoes and a glossy hat, too. Under his hat his hair was newly cut and he was freshly-shaven. All in all he looked a gentleman, which was odd, since he went to meet two prostitutes.

In fairness to Bytheway, the profession of the women had not been explained to him. Woodhouse had merely asked to introduce him to two women who wanted to make his acquaintance. He had asked this favour because, as he said, how often might young women meet a chief clerk? Indeed, they were quite mad to hear about the banking system and the heavy responsibility which reposed in him.

Bytheway wanted to believe this flattery, and as he entered Woodhouse's lodgings he was almost gallant. The two ladies were very respectable; each wore a day dress with puffed-out sleeves and each was very pleasing, smelling of lavender and rustling as she moved. One was black haired and one blonde, though both wore her hair in a coil. Bytheway found an absurd pleasure in the jaunty angle of each woman's hat, which in each case was accentuated by a white feather.

Woodhouse poured tea and a conversation began about the bank.

'Tell me, Mr Bytheway,' said Miss Taplin, the blonde woman, 'is the accounting system which you use in the bank a terribly complex matter? I've often thought how very clever one must be to undertake such a business.'

She looked at him, turning her head to the side. She was about twenty-three with good skin, blue eyes and a fine, straight nose. She had red, moist lips too, turned up at the corners.

'Yes,' said Bytheway, flushing, looking pleased. 'I may say with justice that it is.' He took a draught of his strange-tasting tea and went on to talk, at some length, about banking, all of which the woman absorbed with the greatest interest. The other woman, Miss Brown, asked him a similar question. She was older, perhaps thirty-five years old, he would guess, with violet eyes and dark brows over them. Bytheway was arrested by her eyes, but to look at her produced a curious breathlessness in him, and his heart raced, so that he gabbled, only saying half he meant to say about the bank. Once again his tea tasted strange, but he took refuge in it.

Bytheway was curious about the women; for example, they were so alluring but Miss Taplin's diction reminded him of a ham actress. Miss Brown, conversely, had a well-to-do, clipped pronunciation. He began to wonder if either woman was of irreproachable character, and yet Miss Brown was so respectable. There was a silence, and then Woodhouse, who had been sitting bolt upright, with his hands in his lap, said, 'Do tell us, Mr Bytheway, about the method by which you reconcile the monies of the bank at the end of the day's trading. I'm sure that the ladies would find it most instructive.'

There was another silence. Bytheway opened his mouth, but of a sudden there was a blast of laughter from Woodhouse and the women. Woodhouse nearly fell from his chair, and Bytheway looked at him, at them, open mouthed.

'Oh stop it, Horace,' said the dark-haired Annie. 'You're really most unkind.'

The sound of her spoon stirring her tea was her only further comment, but Floss, the blonde woman, shrieked like a pig having its throat cut.

'Bless 'im!' Where was her proper pronunciation now, and where was Woodhouse's loyalty, tact, common decency? He was laughing so much that tears ran down his face.

Then something occurred which was unexpected. Annie reached out, ran her hand down Bytheway's cheek and smiled. 'Please don't concern yourself,' she said. In that moment his embarrassment was forgotten. He forgot Woodhouse and Floss and what he did there. His confusion produced another smile in Annie, especially when he looked at Woodhouse. Firstly, Woodhouse seemed to be drunk and secondly, Floss was now sitting on Woodhouse's knee. Furthermore, Floss began to undress. She took off her dress, and her crinoline petticoat followed, until all she wore was a cotton chemise, low cut. She drew this up as she took her place again on Woodhouse's knee, and as she did so he saw the fall of her white, full breasts and the cleavage between them.

'Madam,' he said inanely. Entranced, Bytheway noticed the turn of Floss's legs above her stocking tops.

'Give him a drink,' said Woodhouse, curtly.

From nowhere, Annie produced a bottle of spirits and tipped some into Bytheway's already spiked tea. The tea was now disgusting, but at Annie's gentle bidding he sipped it, and then, encouraged by a smile, tipped back the cup. It was then that he noticed that Annie was standing over him. She had her legs apart and, as he watched, she hauled up her dress over her head. All the impedimenta were removed until, like her friend, she stood only in her chemise with her stockings under it. Also like her friend, her breasts were full and her chemise hung lightly on them, so that her motion in taking off her hat seemed to run through her breasts and, as it did so, ran through him. Something else thrilled him, too. He hated himself for it but it thrilled him: he could see the press of her nipples through the cotton of her underwear. He stared, part terrified, and yet partly as though she had him enthralled. She was so beautiful.

Woodhouse and Floss disappeared into the other room, Woodhouse's bedroom. In so much haste that they did not even close the door, almost at once they began to wrestle on the bed.

'I'm at your service, Mr Bytheway,' said Annie. 'Horace has paid for it.'

Bytheway got up. He was taller than she was, her shoulders were narrow and he felt somehow manly beside her. He raised his hands, wanting despite himself to put them to her pert breasts. 'I cannot,' he said. 'I'm not a tomcat on a wall. I don't mean to be rude, dear Madam.'

'Come along,' she coaxed, and lifted up her chemise, and there the light from the daylight outside showed her to him. Her large breasts swept round and up to her pert nipples; the turn of her hips, her dark, coarse pubic hair and the pink, round flesh above her stocking tops spoke to him, and he could not answer: he was undone. He was an animal indeed, and before he knew they were fumbling at each other. There was some clashing of teeth, some wrestling as they tripped over her abandoned dress, but she pushed him away.

'No. No. Forgive me,' she said. 'I can't. I'm sorry. So sorry.'

Mr Bytheway was caught somewhere between the gentleman and the beast as he watched Annie begin to gather up her clothes.

'So sorry,' she said.

In the other room the bed's headboard began to bang, bang, bang.

'Please don't concern yourself,' he said. It was Annie now who was embarrassed. Bytheway felt sorry for her as she frantically began to dress.

'I'm so sorry,' she repeated. 'I suppose that you must think very badly of me. I'm new to this, Mr Bytheway. I didn't mean to offend you.'

'No, no,' he said, raising his hands and putting them on her breasts by mistake. 'No, pardon me! I'm sure that we both think it is for the best, now we are collected.'

'Yes,' she said.

'Quite,' he said.

'Indeed.'

The silence in which they sat began to extend. A clock on the wall began to count the quiet out. Woodhouse's bedboard also marked out time. In the other room Woodhouse sometimes turned uppermost, showing a dessicated prune of a bottom; sometimes Floss sat astride him, turning her pear shape to them, and a bottom which would have done credit to a pony.

'May I offer you some tea?' said Annie.

'Hoo-hoo-hoo-hooo.'

'Yes, thank you,' said Bytheway. 'That would be most kind.'

'Aaawooo!'

'Perhaps a little sugar may mask the taste of the alcohol in the tea?'

'Yes, thank you.'

'Oooooh. Ah! Ah! Ah!'

'How inclement the weather is at the moment.'

'Yes.'

'Aaarch-aarch-aaarch.'

Suddenly Annie put her hands to her face, covered her eyes and laughed. She laughed quite freely, showing her good teeth, and her eyes, as before, were kind to him. She even dabbed a tear away. Once again she very prettily offered him a drink, which he refused, although she poured whisky for herself and drank it speedily. Bytheway watched as she had another drink. It was odd, but despite everything she remained, somehow, respectable and beautiful, just as before. Now, without embarrassment, she looked at him and he at her. As he looked he thought perhaps he could see a trace of something. If she had a taste for drink perhaps it was that, but her face was beginning to fray a little at the edges, and her eyes told a story, although what that might be he could not say. Somehow he gained a little confidence and heard himself say something.

'I've recently lost my faith.'

'Oooooooh.'

She looked at him. Just as before her eyes grew warm. 'You're a strange man,' she said. 'Uncommon, I mean.' Her smile cupped the corners of her mouth. She looked like a duchess in a painting. 'Does it trouble you?'

'Oooooooooooh.'

'Yes,' he said, 'Deeply. Here I am,' he said. ' Chief clerk, drinking to the bitterest drops from the cup of sin.'

'With me!' She laughed, showing her good teeth and, as before, the violet eyes were amused and kind.

'I'm sorry!' Bytheway was horrified. He drew his brows together and looked quite pained but she stopped him.

'No need,' she said.

There was a moment of concord between them, though neither said anything for a second.

'Let's hope that it returns to you,' she said at last.

Just then there was a banging at the door. Bytheway jumped, as did Annie. 'Mr Woodhouse! Mr Woodhouse! What are you doing in there?'

It was Mrs Pooler, landlady to Woodhouse and a customer of the bank. She was a stickler for rules, and pointed out, through the door, the regulations that applied to young ladies and to 'goings on'. 'I will not have fornication in this house,' she shouted. 'I shall tell Mr Bytheway! I shall tell Mr Deacon!'

As if to ward off the evil that was being done under her roof, Mrs Pooler commenced upon a hymn:

'Thresh the wheat, Lord, Sift the chaff, Lord
And cast it to the fire,

Burn the tares, Lord, Sort the weeds, Lord
And may we never tire.'

There was a final drawn-out moan, which prompted a louder rendition of the hymn, before Woodhouse, sweating like a horse, tumescent and covering his manly pride with a hand, hopped over to the door, pulling on his trousers one-handed as he came.

'How dare you, Mrs Pooler!' he shouted through the door. Behind him Floss, like an actress between scenes, bounced round the room, trying to put all her clothes back on at once, or so it seemed. Annie fussed round her, and round them both Bytheway flitted like an imp, desperately indicating that Woodhouse should not say that he was there.

Bang, bang, bang came the summons once again. 'Open this door immediately! Mr Bytheway will hear of this. You will not carry on in this house. Cats and dogs: like cats and dogs, I say. Like frogs in the springtime. Disgusting! Open it, I say. Open it in the name of the Queen!'

'This is an outrage!' shouted Woodhouse, turning and frantically pointing at the window. The pummelling started again at the door.

It was fortunate that a French window opened into the front garden and, indeed, that Woodhouse had rooms on the ground floor. The ladies would not have been able to squeeze through a sash window in their crinolines, or to slide down a drainpipe. As it was, the opening proved only just wide enough, but they passed out into the garden and Bytheway followed them. The hammering on the door continued, but they serenely strolled across the grass towards the road. Hardly had they reached it when they heard an increased commotion and heated words: Woodhouse had opened the door. Gaining the pavement without anyone seeing their escape, they glanced around, respectable once more. No one was watching, and all of a sudden they began to laugh, the three of them almost howling with merriment.

Thereafter they walked on towards the city, and when they reached the cathedral, on the left, Bytheway did look this time. He stared at the cathedral with a sort of insolence, buoyed up as he was with a woman on either arm, but then thought better of it and looked away. He thought no more about the church, and they continued to the railway station where, in good time, the ladies were handed by Bytheway onto a train. Lastly he looked deep into Annie's violet eyes, and then turned and walked away. He was now a rascal indeed.

Chapter Twelve

The first warning about the bank reached Deacon from the lips of Woodhouse's landlady. He was strolling along St John Street when Mrs Pooler accosted him, backing him into a gateway. So close did she press him that they looked like lovers forgetting themselves in the broad open day. He glanced about him nervously.

'Mr Deacon! Mr Deacon! Stay, sir, stay. Have you any conception of what a monster you employ in your bank?'

Spittle picked at Deacon's face. He flinched slightly but viewed her carefully. Under her small, sloping bonnet with its high, pointed brim, her eyes blazed. Stocky, short, pug-nosed, Mrs Pooler reminded Deacon of a bulldog pup. 'Of whom do you speak?'

'Young Mr Woodhouse!'

Deacon was on his way to a meeting of the Conduit Lands Trust. He shuffled his weight and showed the whites of his eyes, everything about him suggesting gross impatience. He was not far short of being rude, but managed to assemble his features into something suggesting good manners. Public confidence in the bank was critical. If he lost the trust of the city then he would be ruined. This was why he paid Bytheway so much. 'What's he done, Mrs Pooler?'

'Slaked his lust under my roof!'

One of Deacon's gingery eyebrows raised a little; one of his round cheeks dropped. He stroked at the ginger ruff of hair beneath his jaw line. 'Go on, Madam.'

'There's an explicit prohibition, Mr Deacon, of young ladies coming to visit young men under my roof, unless they're properly chaperoned. Young Mr Woodhouse entertained a woman in his rooms yesterday afternoon and, I must tell you,' Mrs Pooler glanced to her left and to her right, her voice rising in a crescendo, 'he, he, he ...'

'Yes, Madam, yes,' encouraged Deacon.

'Ravished her!'

'What?'

'Don't force me to say it again!'

Deacon had put aside any thought of the Conduit Lands Trust. He tugged and tugged at the hair under his chin. Mrs Pooler was pleased. There was a sort of wistful expression on Deacon's face that she imagined was an indication of his shock – but he was picturing a fine, strapping woman astride young Woodhouse.

Mrs Pooler rubbed her hands and shifted from foot to foot.

'I presume,' Deacon said, gulping, putting aside a shocking image of Woodhouse in his lust, 'that you protested to him?'

'I did. I banged upon the door.'

'And did you see the woman? She was a fleshy, brazen woman, I'll be bound.'

'No.' Mrs Pooler frowned. 'The vixen had flown by the time I gained admittance. He came to the door, blown like a horse, sweat on his brow, and claimed to have been performing physical exercise on his bed, hence the noise of the headboard and the sound of his exertions.'

Deacon screwed his face up and considered the matter. The image of two great fat buttocks flashed briefly across his mind. 'Mrs Pooler, I shall go directly to the bank to deal with this matter.'

'Thank you! After all, am I safe under my own roof with such a lecher in the house? I tell you, Mr Deacon, and you may tell Mr Woodhouse if you wish, that I've taken to keeping a saucepan under my bed lest the monster molest me in the night. And do not forget the maxim *Falsus in uno, falsus in omnibus*: false in one thing, false in everything. Good afternoon.'

'Good afternoon.' Deacon watched as she trotted off with her nose aloft. In her three-quarter-length cloak over her flounced skirt she had a triangular silhouette, very natty; and she was equally fastidious in crossing the road, negotiating horse manure as though picking her way among flowers.

When he reached the bank, Deacon flung the door open, setting the bell jangling. Woodhouse jumped and Bytheway flushed, though both were working at the time. There was a quick exchange of glances.

'Mr Bytheway.'

'Yes, sir?'

'Please come into my office immediately.'

Bytheway arranged his ledgers, buying time to clear his thoughts. Both he and Woodhouse had risen when Deacon entered, and both had bowed, but there had been no courtesy on Deacon's part.

Woodhouse turned his head to his work, then watched the retreating backs until the door shut behind them. As ever, the shutting of the door insulted him. What Bytheway was fit to hear so too was he. He was further irritated because he sensed they were talking about him, and began to speculate. Could it be that Deacon had discovered the theft? Woodhouse considered running to his lodgings, grabbing some necessaries and escaping. In the confusion perhaps he might escape by train and get away to a port. His heart pounded. Perhaps he might blame it all on Bytheway. He rehearsed a shocked and horrified expression. 'How could you say it was me, Mr Bytheway? Oh, you snake in the grass.' While he refined his performance he moved nearer the door, but try as he might he could hear not so much as a word from the office.

The conversation behind the office door was deep and earnest.

'Tell me, George, about Woodhouse.' Deacon stroked at the whiskers under his chin and paced up and down. 'Mrs Pooler tells me that he had a woman in his rooms. I hardly care if he had a woman there; he's a young man, and I was vigorous once. I don't know if you were ever young but I was young. However, I do care about the bank. Public confidence is everything, everything! Is Woodhouse a liability? Can we trust him?'

'I believe that we may trust him.' Bytheway was calm and serious. He could see that Deacon was agitated, so he was deliberately unemotional. He stroked his chin with the backs of his fingers, frowning, not wanting Deacon to think that he took the matter lightly. 'Mrs Pooler is, I might say in candour, a busybody. I don't believe that people generally give credence to her.'

'There's something else,' said Deacon. His eyes burned brightly, and he moved closer. Bytheway waited, his heart racing. 'There's a narrowness in Woodhouse's features, a pinched quality, which I believe may betoken dishonesty. What do you think of that?' Deacon had become interested in the work of Dr Gall of Vienna, who had founded the 'science' of phrenology – alleging that character, attributes and shortcomings were deducible by the shape of a person's skull.

'I think that phrenology has no basis in fact,' said Bytheway. 'It's no more than humbug, sir, in my opinion.'

'Ha!' said Deacon. He pointed at Bytheway. 'Ha.' Bytheway a sceptic ... On another day he might have made more of it, but he waved the distraction away.

Bytheway watched as his employer began pacing back and forth. 'I don't believe that we need to investigate his work, check his reckoning and bookwork, or surprise him in any way, sir. I think it would be completely unnecessary. I can vouch for Mr Woodhouse.' Bytheway was shocked by the ease with which the lie slipped out.

At this point something happened between them. Mr Deacon stopped, considered what Bytheway had said, and accepted it. 'You see, George, how I value your opinion?'

Bytheway bowed. He was grateful, even moved, but he felt as though someone had taken hold of his guts – as if someone had taken the skein of his innards and was playing it out yard by yard.

'To be sure, I made too much of it.' Bytheway listened attentively but struggled even to look at him. 'Now I think of it, there is a quality to Mrs Pooler's face that may denote hysteria. As you say, people know her to be a tittle-tattle. I think we may overlook this report.'

Deacon was now very late for his meeting. He took his gold pocket watch out and looked at it, made a hasty farewell and dashed out. The door closed behind him with a crash: the interview was over.

Immediately Woodhouse was flitting round Bytheway like a fairy, making circular gestures with his hands. 'What is it? What? Tell me.'

Bytheway, unable to say anything, could do nothing more than sit down at his desk and raise his hands to his face, thinking as he did so.

'What did he say?'

Bytheway ignored Woodhouse. He heard his entreaties but could not think of him; he was thinking of their theft, and whether they might retreat from it. Finally he raised his face from his hands and looked at Woodhouse. 'We've got to give it up.'

'Why' said Woodhouse. 'What did he want? Does he know? He can't.'

'No,' said Bytheway. 'Because we're still here and not in the cells. He wondered if you were to be trusted. I had to vouch for you. For you!'

Woodhouse's long face took on a lopsided grin. 'Don't be rude, Mr B.' He returned to his desk and lent on it, crossing his arms, a gold watch chain showing in the waistcoat of his rather too smart three-piece lounge suit. 'Was it that witch Mrs Pooler?'

'It was.' Bytheway shook his head, frowning. 'She told Mr Deacon that you had a woman in your rooms, and he was worried that there might be a scandal that would cause a loss of public confidence in the bank.'

'Lucky he didn't know the chief clerk was there. You spilled the milk, didn't you, George? At least you tried. I saw you fumbling, old man, until the lady thought better of it.'

'We have to stop it!' Bytheway struck his desk. 'If we stop now we may be able to hide our tracks, but if we go on we shall be caught. You realise that, don't you? We shall be caught.'

'You've changed your tune.' Woodhouse looked at Bytheway in the way that he looked at savers who only kept a pittance in the bank. 'I thought you wanted to punish old Deacon.'

'He trusts me!' said Bytheway.

'Oh. He's a fool then, isn't he?'

Bytheway put his hands to his face in a sort of reply.

'I'm rather enjoying myself,' said Woodhouse. 'I'm not lily-livered like you. The fact that the old man suspected something gives a bit of a fizz to it, don't you think? I'm making too much money to give it up. If we can keep it going a little while longer I'll be away. Deacon won't catch me; don't worry about that.'

'I'm not in the least worried about that!' Bytheway stood to his full five feet eleven inches – but Woodhouse was six feet one and looked down at him as one would a child. 'I have a name, a reputation, and he trusts me. People too, our customers, could lose everything, everything! I have sold my soul for this. What came over me?'

'Have a tot of brandy from The Swan,' said Woodhouse, 'and get a grip of yourself, man. You'll be blubbing next.' He returned to his desk and said nothing more. Whatever he was doing, whether it was work or not, he was busy, and he meant to imply that any talk of giving up was over.

The silence which set in at this point was long lasting. It was a kind of pregnant silence, with the heavy sense of something unsaid. Whenever the clerks were busy or displeased with each other the clock seemed loud, and so it did now. The two men sat, intensely aware of each another but saying nothing. As they went on, however, Bytheway began to forget Woodhouse. His hands did his bidding, and part of his mind orchestrated his work, but he was thinking of the changes to his once orderly life. For one thing, he lamented his faith. Why did he so yearn for faith but, angry or not, he wanted it? Often in bed he called its name, listening for it in the dead of the night and, sometimes, thought that it whispered his name, too. Perhaps he might liken it to a stray dog which had once followed him. He had turned to drive it away, and it shied, but afterwards it began again to track him. In a similar way he could not drive off the dog of faith although, at the same time that he rejected it, he yearned for it.

Bytheway began to count all the changes to his life. The loss of his faith was change enough, he thought, but he had also become a thief and a discriminating investor. There was something else too. His hand still carried the impress of Annie's flesh; he could feel her breasts and the turn of her smooth skin under his hand. He was drunk with the thought of her, drunk as those who tumbled from the pubs and fought in the gutter, who sang in the streets, who went home having spent all their money, so their children went hungry. A truth was dawning upon him, a truth that was terrible to tell, terrifying and yet wonderful, wonderful beyond expression. The world had shifted and he was running towards something, running so fast that his legs could hardly carry him. That something was the vision of Annie, and again, even now, as he began to think of her everything else was crowded from his mind. He determined to see her again, by whatever means, as soon as he possibly could.

Chapter Thirteen

Bytheway was attentive to Carney and often went to see him, as did other people, but Carney wanted no one really, save his housekeeper and Bytheway. His world had shrunk to the confines of his bed and his private thoughts. He had also become sensitive to noise, and light, and so anyone who visited him had to whisper in a sort of twilight. Sometimes visitors had to share, to some degree, in the humiliations of his illness; for example, when he had foul bedlinen. His housekeeper, who was his greatest solace, tried to keep him clean, but occasionally there was an unpleasant smell in his airless, dark room.

For the above reasons, Bytheway had to steel himself when he visited his friend. In fact, he did not enjoy these visits but, like it or not, he went almost daily. Today he approached Carney's lodgings, an old house in Dam Street, and began to ready himself. Dam Street was busy, as always, but as he drew near a hearse passed him, pulled by a black horse. On top of the hearse was Mr Blackstock, the undertaker, who recognised Bytheway. The hearse stopped.

'He's gone, Mr Bytheway.' Blackstock had a face like a bad-tempered bulldog, all chops and fierce little eyes. He put his hat back on his head and gave it a tap. 'A bad do.'

Bytheway stood in the light of the late afternoon, smelling the horse, hearing the jangle of its harness, the scrape of one of its hooves on the cobbled road. Everything was so earthy and real, and yet he felt unreal. The news shocked him, as if Carney had never been ill. He continued to stand in the road, in his top hat and shiny shoes, long coat and woollen trousers, so respectable, but fighting to avoid a public show of feeling. That would never do. He was sufficiently troubled, however, not to notice that Blackstock had gone, leaving him standing in the road. He began to attract attention, so collected himself and hurried to Carney's lodgings, where he found Mrs Reed, Carney's housekeeper and comforter.

Mrs Reed opened the door and invited him in. 'I'm so sorry,' said Bytheway. This might have seemed a strange thing to say, as Carney no more than lived in her house, but over the course of his friend's illness Bytheway had noticed the bond between Carney and Mrs Reed, who was a widow. She had been party to all the inconveniences and humiliations of Carney's illness, and yet had never flinched.

There was a great faded prettiness about Mrs Reed; her fine cheekbones had become subsumed in the spread which had enlarged her all over, but her eyes remained very fine and her brows were black, although her hair was otherwise streaked with grey. In her cotton cap and short-sleeved linen dress, which showed her arms, she looked every inch a working woman, especially in her linen apron, and she lacked the shape of a fine lady, wanting a boned bodice or stiffened petticoats which gave more fashionable women their prized silhouettes. Even so, Bytheway was immensely impressed with her.

'Thank you so much for all your care of Charles.'

Mrs Reed nodded and thanked him. She had been in this situation of loss before and reverted to a sort of stoicism which had served her well in the past. Despite this she sometimes cried a little. He and she stood looking at each other, across her bare table in her dark and cramped little room.

'There was something,' she said at last, 'which Charlie wanted me to tell you.' She swallowed hard a moment. 'He wanted you to know that he died a Christian.' She stopped a moment and then went on. 'He was becoming hard to hear but he tried so hard, Mr Bytheway, to tell me. He said that he died in the "perfect hope of his redemption", that was it, and he wanted you to be of good heart.'

She said this and smiled and then, begging pardon, began upon some job of a domestic nature, which she did because it had to be done and no one else would do it. Bytheway stood and watched her, listening to a catch in her breathing. He turned to go, but then asked permission to visit Carney's room, which she gave him. Inside the room everything was just as it had been, save the bed was bare and the curtains were open to the day. The window was also open to let the air in, and blow away any thought of death, but otherwise there were so many of Carney's things there, just as if he had gone out, briefly. Bytheway sat beside the bed and wondered if the splendour of a new life had begun for his friend, one without pain, in the everlasting kingdom. Softly, Bytheway called Carney's name and, like a rabbit listening for danger, raised his head and listened lest Carney answer him, but there was no answer. In the room was a deafening silence and a great sense of the ordinary. Despite the silence Bytheway felt encouraged, for the first time in a long time, and thanked Carney, saying it out loud, lest his friend might hear him, and then quietly left the room and went about his way.

Chapter Fourteen

Carney's funeral was surprising in that so many women attended, more than one might have expected Carney to know. The church was full. Another surprise was that Deacon closed the bank and took it upon himself to lead the tributes. He had, he said, paid a 'pretty penny' for the funeral, and duly occupied the 'best' pew, relegating Carney's family to one row further back. There had been a look on Deacon's face that had not invited challenge. He had folded his arms when the verger suggested that he might move, pugged his jaw up and grumbled 'Humbug! Did they attend poor Carney when he was ill?' Thereafter he had maintained this demeanour through all the prayers and responses.

The service went on, almost like a dream of sorts, but eventually they found themselves on the path to the grave. There were some more rituals around the pit and they stood miserably watching as the coffin was lowered into the ground. The words of the service, however, were beautiful. Bytheway felt encouraged, even hopeful, but compared the ephemeral words with the damp soil from the hole, which would soon be cast back into it. All the mourners, it seemed, were reflective, and so they stood, pondering, while the service was concluded, until it came time to leave their brother Charles Carney in the ground. After the coffin had been interred, and after the mourners had dropped little stones on it, and after they had drifted away, Deacon stood with Woodhouse and Bytheway on the edge of the grave. The three men stood wordless and each one seemed unaware of the others. At last, however, Deacon turned to them both.

'Gentlemen, you were both good to poor Carney. I know that you've not the resources that I enjoy, but you did what you could. I respect that. Even you, Mr Woodhouse, behaved well, and I thank you. You, George, in particular deserve notice.' Deacon bunched his cheeks up, licked his lips and tried to say something. 'You're a good man, George.'

This produced a fit of coughing which was shared equally between the three men. Deacon also shook his round cheeks but dragged his eyes up to those of Bytheway. Poor Deacon. It seemed that making this speech was a tremendous effort. Solemnly he took Woodhouse's hand and shook it, then shook Bytheway's hand. Bytheway shuffled and blushed, Deacon blushed and shuffled, and Woodhouse seemed shocked.

'I believe,' said Deacon, taking a huge breath, 'that I've wronged you, George. I apologise. There, I have said it.' He reached out and took Bytheway's limp hand again, while Woodhouse watched as he might have done if a horse had passed by dancing a waltz with a cow. 'How good it is, gentlemen,' added Deacon, to lighten the moment, 'to be out into the open air, away from all that cant inside the church. Oh, I was forgetting that you, Bytheway, swell their number. Well, more fool you!' And with that he rammed his hat on his head and was off, as if the birds of the air and the beasts of the field and all else that drew breath owed him their allegiance, leaving his clerks to watch him as he went. The two men observed him for some time, until he was out of earshot.

'Even you, Mr Woodhouse, behaved well,' sneered Woodhouse, doing a fine impression of Deacon. 'Impudence! And to be sure, Mr Bytheway,' he added, still in Deacon's voice, 'in so far as embezzlers are considered you are one of the best of men.'

Bytheway waved this facetiousness away. 'He does have a regard for me,' he said. 'Mr Deacon apologised to me.'

Woodhouse sighed. 'You will quite make me blub if you continue to be so soppy.'

'No!' said Bytheway, 'He does have a regard for me.'

'Please!' Woodhouse bunched his cheeks and squinted at Bytheway. 'He was quite the gentleman for a moment or so, wasn't he? Very appreciative, complimentary, and then he had to spoil it. Have you forgotten already? What was it Deacon said?' He impersonated Deacon again. 'Well, more fool you.' The pompous old devil! I want to know what happened to his wife and children. There is something fishy about that, Mr B., you mark my words.'

'What are you suggesting?'

Woodhouse glanced over his shoulder. 'I tell you: he did them in.'

'No!'

Woodhouse winced at Bytheway's innocence, then changed topic; he had other fish to fry. 'There is no going back, George. Once a thief, always a thief. There can be no redemption.'

'I am not a thief!'

'Oh,' said Woodhouse. 'Have you forgotten the notes which we divided between us only yesterday?' With that he turned and went, without so much as another word.

Bytheway was left on his own, save for his friend Carney, who lay in the ground; but it was a poor comfort that Bytheway drew from Carney being near. Indeed, he gave every impression of being in pain. For a moment he seemed wretched enough to climb in on top of Carney, but he collected himself. Picking up some little stones from among the soil around the grave, he dropped them into the pit. In truth, however, Bytheway was no longer thinking of Carney, but some sense of decency restored his friend to his mind, and before he left he took a last look. He noted the polished wood, the brass plate, the depth of the hole, the soil that would soon be thrown into it, and then said something, whether a prayer or a goodbye, and left without looking back. As he left a blackbird sang over the grave, and Bytheway thought he would leave the last word to him.

Chapter Fifteen

Deacon was not averse to trading favours, and in this way procured an invitation to visit John Brisker. Brisker was a rich man and Deacon hoped to persuade him to invest in his bank. As Deacon approached Brisker's home, his anticipation mounted. The property had ramparts around it and was accessible only through a gatehouse, which suggested that Brisker had treasure inside. An alarm rang in Deacon, which always sounded when he detected money.

The bell jangled at the door and a man came to answer it, a small man, with fierce eyes, who demanded his business.

'Mr Brisker? I'm John Deacon, sir, of J.W. Deacon, bankers of Lichfield.'

Had Deacon trodden in something foul; had he rolled in excrement like a dog; was he a molester of animals or children? He had done none of these things, but this little man looked at him with something like disgust. The apples shone in Deacon's cheeks.

'John Brisker,' said the man at last. 'Pardon. Come in, sir.'

This said, he turned and went. Deacon looked back towards his carriage and hesitated before entering, but at last followed. Brisker led him into a room but then ignored him.

'Papers,' said Brisker. 'Papers.'

As Deacon watched, Brisker emptied successive drawers onto the floor. What should Deacon do? He could not sit until invited, but impeded Brisker who moved between cabinets. Brisker also confused Deacon by talking to himself, so that Deacon did not know to whom Brisker spoke. Once, Deacon failed to respond when Brisker had spoken to him.

'The man's deaf!' said Brisker loudly. 'Deaf as a post.' The apples glowed again in Deacon's cheeks at this. Thereafter, whenever Brisker mumbled anything Deacon spoke up: 'I beg your pardon?'

Finally Brisker stood still and the two men faced each other. Mr Brisker had a pinched quality: pinched in face, expression and frame; but otherwise he had short, side-parted hair and an odd, bustling way of walking. He had a staccato way of talking, too.

'My wife, coming down soon, sir, I assure you, unpardonably rude, my apologies. So, I hear good reports of your bank, sir. We'll talk more, sir. May I offer you refreshment?' Deacon next took opportunity to look round the room, which he professed to admire. The room had a piano, windows overlooking the garden and walls which were dotted with pictures, including one, over the fireplace, of a handsome, dark-eyed woman. The woman had most arresting eyes.

'My wife,' said Brisker, 'Mine. Where is the woman?' His brows met over his eyes and he stamped off calling – shouting, one might have said – up the stairs.

'Mrs Brisker, I want you! Are you coming down? Mr Deacon's waiting to meet you.'

Brisker lingered, then returned to the room where Deacon stood waiting. The men looked at each other.

'Have you any children, sir?'

Deacon was startled. 'I regret ...'

'Nor we.' Deacon, being interrupted, grew red, his face echoing the colour of his patterned waistcoat.

'My wife, sir,' continued Brisker, 'has been barren these fifteen years. No children.' Brisker looked left, Brisker looked right. With a gesture he drew Deacon forward. 'A man wants an heir, sir. I'll tell you, sir, gratis, lest your own woman is barren, huh, huh, huh. I've obliged my wife to eat gruel in the morning. It may make her fertile, sir. The water treatment too, sir. I've in mind to send her to Malvern. There is a doctor there who has refined the therapeutic use of water bathing. It's most efficacious. The fellow has various methods, sir, of applying water to invalids. I've in mind for Mrs Brisker the douche, in which the patient stands under a sudden fall of cold water. It stimulates the nervous system, sir, as you might imagine.'

'Indeed.'

' It may make her fertile,' said Brisker.

'Or consumptive.'

'I know best, I think; and she'll do what she's told. It may make her fertile. A man wants an heir.' A joke seemed to flicker in Brisker. Deacon waited. 'To tell the truth, sir, I've not mentioned it to her yet, but she shall go!'

There, he had provided repartee; it was now Deacon's turn. Perhaps Brisker was shy, but he seemed now to have nothing to say, although he anticipated a reply: his dark eyes fastened on Deacon like leeches. 'Huh, huh, huh,' he murmured. There was a silence which began to extend. Deacon had not the slightest idea what to say, so perhaps, therefore, he fell back upon a favourite topic.

'You're a discriminating man, sir; perhaps you'd be interested in this watch. Gold, sir. It cost me a pretty penny! Indeed, it is no idle boast that ...'

'Huh, huh,' snorted Brisker. He used this expletive to tease out more information and it passed, too, for enthusiasm in him. All the while Brisker perused Deacon as if he meant to eat him. Clearly Deacon was a man of means. Brisker next admired Deacon's carriage.

'Huh, huh, huh,' he said to every wonder about it.

Deacon began to talk of his horses, of which he was very proud.

'To business,' said Brisker.

Just for a moment, Deacon thought of leaving. He did not like being interrupted. He stood pondering at the window, but then noticed someone. It was the dark-eyed woman from the portrait. Immediately, Deacon joined Brisker and they sat down at last to business.

Unknown to Brisker, his wife was passing along the carriage drive toward the road. She was in haste and did not walk but scurried, wearing a cloak which, in the fashion of the time, gave her a triangular shape. If only Bytheway might have seen her. She had dark brows and violet eyes, which Bytheway remembered well; and so, it seemed, that Bytheway's 'Miss Brown' was also Mrs Brisker.

Annie – her first name really was Ann – glanced at the windows, but the men were busy. When Brisker missed her she would be in trouble, although he had never yet assaulted her. Annie was going into Walsall, where she was known at several of the town's pubs. In fact, when she got to town she would meet Floss and her circle, taking a place among them. These rude, unlettered people were unfit company for her, as the world would have it, and she disgraced herself by being among them, but they accepted her. Of course, it had its dangers. How she had stooped to prostitution she hardly knew: drink, the will of one publican and anger towards her husband had made her do it, she supposed, as well as disgust at her disgrace, being known, as she was, as a 'scandalous woman'. She also suspected her husband of using prostitutes, so what greater revenge than to become one herself? One thing, however: she would not prostitute herself again. The publican/pimp had accepted this, for the moment, and in the meantime she returned to his pub, and others, when she could escape, compelled by loneliness and rebellion.

She knew, of course, that her 'gutter companions', as her husband called them, would seek to exploit her. Once beyond their initial suspicion of her, they had begun to explore her utility to them. Sometimes, however, Annie found among them something which she believed to be friendship, and that one thing made everything worthwhile; together with the drink, which she began to enjoy more than she should. No wonder, then, that Brisker would come and take her home.

When she was clear of the house she stopped a moment, as if she had been deposited there and had no idea where to go. There was something woebegone about her, like a cat turned out of home. She was flushed too, partly from her escape and partly from the brandy she had taken. The colour drew attention to her eyes, with that quality in them that Bytheway had noticed in Lichfield, which suggested pain and that she had a tale to tell, if anyone would but hear it. In her haste, her hair had come loose and two strands trailed down her face. The black against her skin showed the turn of her cheekbones and intensified her dejected appearance. Likewise, there was something incongruous in her mouth which hung, it seemed, upon the makings of a smile.

Annie did not feel much inclined towards levity at that moment. From somewhere about her she produced a flask and drank something. Blinking, and after a little shudder, she set off on her way towards a pub. Even before Deacon left, Brisker would discover that she was gone and set out, once again, to look for her.

Chapter Sixteen

Deacon was a busy man. He had interests in all sorts of factories, collieries, and the railway company, and sat on the Board of Guardians of the workhouse, among other things. One of these other things was the bank, but whenever he was there something soon called him away. On these occasions he generally said where he went, but once a month he would not give his whereabouts. It was always a Wednesday when he went missing, and Woodhouse imagined that Deacon visited a woman.

One Wednesday afternoon Bytheway and Woodhouse were working when Deacon came through into the public area of the bank. He wore a three-piece lounge suit, narrow tie and shiny shoes. The two clerks glanced at each other.

'At four I shall be at The Swan on a matter of business. Good afternoon, gentlemen.'

'Good afternoon, Mr Deacon.'

The door closed behind him. Woodhouse looked at the clock. It was now short of two: where was Deacon going? Woodhouse tried to watch Deacon, but a customer arrived, and when Woodhouse returned to the window Deacon had gone. At such a time it would have been useful to have possessed second sight. If they could have seen him, Deacon was passing through the crowds. It was a market day and people filled the streets. Deacon was civil enough but kept on, and now Woodhouse's suspicions about him began to seem believable.

Deacon left the market-place and went along Dam Street. From the end of Dam Street he returned the way he had come. There was one clue to his behaviour. Sometimes, in the market-place, he looked about him. Once more he went along Dam Street. He studied the pool in a leisurely way, then retraced his steps. On this last occasion he perused a shop window, again near the market.

'Mr Deacon, how do you do?'

'Ah! Mr Ayres, you startled me, sir.'

Throughout the conversation Deacon shifted. When Mr Ayres left Mr Ruddock came! Deacon spent so long outside the shop that he was finally obliged to buy something. When he left the shop he did so like an ogre emerging from its cave. Plainly disagreeable, he scowled right and left, but at last there was a gap in the passing traffic. Quickly he went up to a door, knocked once and was admitted.

So this was where Deacon went once a month; so close to the bank and so unlikely a place! How Woodhouse and Bytheway would have marvelled to see him there.

Inside the house, Deacon exchanged formalities with an old man. The man and Deacon had a brief, knockabout chat. Neither man enjoyed the conversation, and finally it ended in silence. The formalities over, the old man looked at Deacon. Deacon nodded. Once he wiped at his brow and hands with a handkerchief, then followed Mr Hawkins along a corridor. The floorboards creaked. It was dark inside the house and there was a smell. Deacon did not hide his disgust. The drab, bald, bent little man noted his reaction but did not care. He led Deacon into a room and sat him down. Deacon seemed to expect something; hence, perhaps, he screwed himself up, and it came. Hawkins ran his fingers down Deacon's scalp, down his neck, until they spidered along his shoulders. Suddenly Deacon seemed talkative, but the old man crept round the table, softly, as if attempting to surprise somebody. Finally he took a chair opposite Deacon. There was a moment of waiting. Deacon and Mr Hawkins surveyed each other, then Hawkins peered into a silver bowl, which contained water. So the minutes passed. Tick-tock; tick-tock; tick-tock. A chair creaked. Deacon shifted. Tick-tock; tick-tock; tick-tock. They continued to sit and sit and sit. Tick-tock, tick tock; and then something happened.

'Tell her not to go; tell her not to go; he means ill by her. Tell her not to go ...'

Suddenly Hawkins had the voice of a mouse behind a skirting board, but that voice was then supplanted. His speech changed and became sonorous; almost enough to vibrate through the table and the elbows of Deacon who lent upon it. Then another voice: 'We put to sea in a howling gale out of Plymouth.'

Sometimes these things were unintelligible; sometimes his utterances made sense. Deacon seemed confused.

'I've a young man who particularly wishes to speak to you,' said Hawkins suddenly, in a voice that lifted the hairs on Deacon's neck. 'A young man with a scar across one cheek. He doesn't speak clearly but I see him well. Shall we hear him, Mr Deacon?'

'No!' said Deacon. He tugged at his gingery whiskers. 'No. That does not signify. Another, please.'

Hawkins frowned and passed a hand over the bowl, then settled again. Deacon settled too, in the sense, at least, that he remained seated. Much might be read, however, in his posture; he sat screwed up, like a walnut. How amusing they might have seemed, but Hawkins was in earnest. Deacon, too, remained dogged. He tutted periodically, shook his head, muttered and blinked his eyes but remained seated.

Hawkins began to talk again in a jumble of voices. This time one voice would run into another. With each new offering Deacon frowned until, finally, he asked about his wife. In this moment, at last, he revealed what he did there. Mr Deacon, arch-sceptic, disciple of Darwin, scourge of the Church, was desperate to contact his wife. He wanted forgiveness from her because he had killed her. He had killed his wife and each of their children in turn, one after the other. Sometimes he was desperate to talk of it, to explain how he had murdered them. Some day he must tell somebody about it. He could not bear it. If only his wife might tell him not to torture himself! She did not come forward, however. He had come time and again but she did not come forward. He had no belief in what he did there, but still he came.

They sat some while longer but the spirits became silent, except one voice which intruded on them. A small voice, like a kitten scratching at a door for entry, but nothing else, and eventually the small voice was still. Deacon covered his face with his hands and sank forward onto the table. His back was wet with sweat. He hardly had strength enough to move.

'Mr Deacon', said Hawkins. 'Mr Deacon.'

At length, Deacon looked up. Hawkins eyed him.

'I'm sorry, Mr Deacon, but I've had no luck once again. Do please come another time. One thing, however.' Deacon heaved his eyes up to the watery, spaniel eyes of the old man. 'I sense that someone may be abusing your trust.'

Deacon turned this over in his mind. For a moment he considered the bank – but the last thing he wished to do was suggest that it had even entered his thoughts.

'One of the servants, perhaps?' he said. 'Drinking the whisky again.'

Hawkins seemed unsure, but Deacon jumped up and headed for the door. The man followed him sadly, like an old dog. Very little time was wasted. Deacon took out the old man's fee. For a moment it seemed that he would throw it down and make the old man scrabble for it. He did not. He handed over some coins, and the man took them with a brown, bony hand.

'Good day to you, Mr Hawkins,' said Deacon, as if he wished the very opposite. Hawkins bowed, then opened the door to the bright, spanking day. Deacon absorbed the sunshine as though the want of it had almost killed him. Outside was a pile of horse manure, just deposited. There was a trace of steam rising from the dung and a tang of muck on the air. In that moment he wondered if he had ever seen anything so beautiful. Could there be anything more life affirming, more suggestive of the everyday? The manure might have been lavender water so deeply did Deacon inhale its aroma. He marched off, denouncing Hawkins as a fraud, and swore that he would never visit the house again. He was angry, too, with Bytheway for his religious cant, and angry again with Bytheway for daring to dispute Darwin's truths with him. And so he stamped off, barging through the crowds and quite overcome by a filthy temper.

Chapter Seventeen

One day after work Bytheway and Woodhouse boarded a train and were quickly conducted to Walsall. Oh, the wonders of the modern age! One could travel so quickly, although the journey dragged for Bytheway, who was on his way to see Annie. Annie and Floss were to meet them in a pub, just off the High Street.

Woodhouse was conspicuous in an expensive suit, also a watch and chain. He had the makings of a moustache too, which accentuated the rakish look of his off-centre face. Bytheway was not brash but attempted to walk as a gentleman, back straight and so on. No wonder that they attracted some cat calls.

'Come along, George,' coaxed Woodhouse. 'Pay no attention to the undeserving poor.'

So it was that they proceeded to a tumbledown pub which lent, it seemed, against the angle of the hill. The outside of the building was grimy and the windows black. What did they do here? thought Bytheway, who stopped. Ordinarily he would have avoided the place like a midden. To go inside called for an effort of will, but the promise of Annie encouraged him, and he entered. Woodhouse had already gone in.

'Evening, Bert,' said Woodhouse. He addressed himself to a thickset man with no obvious neck. The man winced but nodded to the corner. Never before had Bytheway been in such a place. The pub stank: of beer, damp, and unwashed people. The unwashed part was pungent enough to shorten the breathing; it was the smell of unclean linen, mixed with sweat. As they went on, Bytheway adjusted to the poor light. The pub was full and even the walls were lined with benches. At intervals were copper-topped tables, which dotted the floor. Bytheway hoped to pass unnoticed, but wherever they went faces turned to them. This watchfulness transmitted itself to him, but the gap he made, pressing into the room, filled behind him and he was subsumed into the crowd, a long way from the door.

They continued to squeeze through the pub until they came to a side room, really no more than an alcove. This was theirs and in it, waiting, were Annie and Floss. Floss rose up and embraced Woodhouse; Annie was more collected. Bytheway flustered. He bowed, of course, but said little. Annie, too, looked bashful, but Bytheway soon found himself under her warm gaze. 'How very nice to see you again, Mr Bytheway,' she said.

In a corner of the room a fight broke out. Albert barged through the crowd and bundled both combatants out into the street.

'I'm very pleased to see you again, Annie,' Bytheway said. It was ludicrous: there they were, in this unmannerly place, and yet she behaved like the mistress of a Knightsbridge drawing room.

Woodhouse took out some money and jangled it between his hands. He listened to it for a moment, then waved a bottle at Albert, in the same action showing four fingers to request so many glasses. Albert signed a response. Woodhouse produced a similar reaction, too, in showing Albert a coin, as one might try to tempt a child.

"Ave yer got a penny or tow fare me, Annie? Arme a bit short.'

An old woman had come forward and begged money. She was largely toothless and chomped as she spoke, sometimes drawing the back of one hand across her mouth. At close quarters, Bytheway realised that this supplicant was barely middle-aged. They looked at one another, then the woman took a seat among them. Bytheway looked at Woodhouse, who looked at him, and Floss seemed intimidated. The person asked for money again. Annie, however, had subsidised her already, and refused to give her more. Silence. The petitioner asked again. 'No!' The woman began to roll back her sleeves. Repeatedly, she made little snorts and grunts too, as if building up her steam. How slowly such moments drag out: the whole evening seemed suspended on a piece of thread. Bytheway watched Annie's eyes harden and her mouth flatten. Just as the conversation around them began to slacken, the woman stomped away. All at once they heard the noise of the pub again. She was gone. This sponger knew better than to importune Annie.

This interruption should perhaps have given them a warning. There were other people in the pub who were more formidable still than this prematurely aged woman, and they might not be so easily deterred. Bytheway thought that they should leave.

'No, no, no,' said Woodhouse. He waved an expansive hand. 'Not at all.' Bytheway shook his head, but Woodhouse extended himself as if before his fire at home. Only his grip around Floss's waist kept him upright at all.

In a strange turn of events, however, something happened which surprised Bytheway, who enjoyed it, against every expectation. Who would have thought it? Afterwards, Woodhouse raised his hand again, to vindicate himself, and smiled a satisfied smile. What occurred was that a man sang. This man was covered in dust. The dust caked his heavy clothing and clogged in his beard. His eyes were red-rimmed, and he coughed, sometimes spitting into a handkerchief, but he sang like an angel. His lungs and clothes alike must have been contaminated, but his voice was wonderful and, in other circumstances, would have earned him high praise and riches on the stage. The singer sang about love, forbidden love, and all the hardened, grimed, care-worn customers of the pub stopped to listen. At the end of the song a tin mug was passed round and people put pennies in it, as Bytheway and all his party were happy to do.

Crash! Bert slammed down some drinks onto their table. 'Cum ter the bar next toime,' he said.

Woodhouse smiled, paid Bert and showed him a sixpence. Finally he surrendered it, as if to say, 'If you wait upon me you may get a sixpence next time too.' Bert chucked the coin aside and pushed his way back through the crowd. They drank up. As they drank, Bytheway noticed how Annie consumed her drink. It was a glass of port and she tipped it back entire.

'Annie!' He might have said more but she lifted a finger. The same steady stare settled on him as she had used with the person begging money.

'You know, Mr Bytheway, George, I don't even like it. One has to persevere, however.'

He knew not to say any more.

The crowd about them began to thin out. There was to be an entertainment, a cock fight, in an upstairs room. Cock fighting was illegal, which made the event irresistible to Woodhouse. Bytheway and Annie wished to leave, but stayed, mistakenly. Had they noticed the whispering about them they might have gone. Woodhouse, however, took out his money and flourished it.

'Put your money away, Horace,' said Bytheway. Woodhouse defied him and held the purse up. This gesture did not go unnoticed. There was a charge of 15d each, and Woodhouse also made a show of funding their entries. 'The best seats, my man, I thank you: on the front row, if you please!'

So it was that they went upstairs. The steps were dry, dirty and unsafe, truth to tell, but they trudged up. At the top was a room with several rows of benches. There were more seats at the back and at the front was some matting, which was stained. There were also some feathers and wicker baskets. From time to time a cock crowed loudly, close at hand.

The downstairs of the pub and this upstairs room contrasted strongly with each other. Downstairs people were safe, if they belonged there and minded their business, although there were still fights. In this upstairs room, however, there was a threatening atmosphere. Bloodlust had mixed with beer and spirits. As Bytheway cast his eyes around he saw manifest greed. In some cases people in rags gambled perhaps their last money in wagers. A fat man in a frock coat took the bets. He had an impassive quality, like a frog who waits in the knowledge that a fly will come to him.

The to-ing and fro-ing continued for some minutes, but at last everyone seemed to be seated. The crowd was ready and a degree of quiet settled upon it, but nothing happened immediately. No one came to initiate the entertainment, although it was not apparent what impeded them. The sense of anticipation was tangible, however, and at length it became obvious where the problem lay.

Around this time, too, Bytheway realised their error in taking the front row. Owing to their position, he and his party could not see behind them. This was unwise in such a place. They were attracting attention too, and what they did not see they could feel. Floss seemed to be a kind of barometer of their position, and seemed to understand their predicament better than her companions. The others in the party fondly imagined that some deference was due to them, but she continued to turn round anxiously. They waited. They waited longer, and then they waited still more. The atmosphere in the room, already impatient, became strange: febrile but mixed with something else. Even Woodhouse chanced the odd look behind him. There could be no doubting that they were unwelcome. Indeed, it seemed that their presence hindered the entertainment. Then suddenly the evening took a turn for the worse. Bert came up and stared at Woodhouse, then a second man joined Bert and another man stood on Bert's other side.

In the sudden stress, Woodhouse dissimulated. To signify his self-possession he spoke to Floss, and joked. His smile resembled washing on a bowed clothes line, but the eyes seldom lie, and little penny candles burned in each of them. Floss wriggled from his arm but, trying for spirit, he spoke to Bert, using the man's name. Somehow this familiarity in the dead quiet of the room fell crashing to the floor, like a pile of pots and pans. It was then that Woodhouse turned to Bytheway, wanting him to take the trial from him. Meanwhile Floss abandoned him, trotting off, hoping for more congenial company. Around the room the sense of something beginning set people to fidgeting and craning their necks to watch. The next scene was not long in coming.

'Con yow speak for 'im, Floss? 'Oo is 'e? Is 'e a copper?'

'Ah know 'im a bit.'

'Ah wunt 'im out. Yow. Out!'

Bert was in motion in a moment. He grabbed Woodhouse by the wrist and lifted him from his seat. The other men joined him, and together they began to bundle Woodhouse up and out. Lifting a hand to protect his face, no more, he caught Bert on the nose.

'Yow villain,' said Bert. Of a sudden, Woodhouse was taken up into a dance, a sort of jig. Round him danced Bert, and the other men with him, and between them Woodhouse sagged and rolled as one man struck him and then another. Poor Woodhouse. He was a rag doll. He tried to speak but a fist stopped his mouth; he tried to beg but a boot cut off his wind; and suddenly the floor rushed at him. There, among the muck and the blood, the hobnail boots moved round him. On the floor he was adrift; the boards moved under him. Sometimes a boot found out the fragile cage of his ribs; sometimes a boot found the space between his ribs and hip, so that the leather buried itself in him, lifting him and forcing some detritus of gunk from his mouth. They would kill him there. They would kill him!

'Leave him be!'

He thought he heard Bytheway's voice. Annie, too, shouted something. Woodhouse curled up, put his hands to his head and then, he would not have wished this for the world, he sobbed. Despite his anger and pride and the sense that Floss was watching, he sobbed, sobbed like a child.

'Leave the boy be!'

Bytheway sprang up, up to his full five feet eleven inches. Bert and the other men wound down their attack, Bert's bull neck turned round. Like a lizard spotting a fly trapped in a web, Bert's eyes settled on Bytheway. At the back and at the sides everyone looked at Bytheway. People stood to gain a better view.

'D'yow wunt some of t' serme?'

The question hung in the air. It bounced off the dirty walls, and the wide white eyes of the company deflected it one to another. Bert waved a meaty fist and waited for an answer.

'I do not, sir! Please, I will now escort this lady from your house and remove the boy.'

This was met initially by silence, like a stone dropped into a well shaft.

'Gid 'im a terst on it, an' all,' said one of the men.

Bert considered the matter. Finally, feet scraping on the boards, he stood aside. He gestured with his thumb towards the stairs.

Bytheway moved across to Woodhouse and eased him onto his feet. 'Come on, Horace.'

Up to this point, Floss had done or said nothing, but she came forward at last and looked at him, rather like someone discovering dog waste on their shoe. He turned two watery eyes on her, but it was hopeless. Floss, nose aloft, slipped under the arm of one of his assailants. A bit more of the stuffing came loose in Woodhouse, and he hung his head as if he looked for something on the floor.

'Come on, old man, come along.'

Bytheway brushed Woodhouse down, straightened his attire, set him right, and with a nod to the stairs set him in motion, then returned to Annie. She was already on her feet.

'That was quite unnecessary, Albert.' She turned two hard eyes on Bert. Her colour was up and her violet eyes gleamed. Bytheway offered his arm, and they followed Woodhouse to the stairs. Behind them came catcalls, and somebody sang a wedding ditty. Then, allowing her to go first, Bytheway stood under the gaze of them all.

'Thank you,' he said. He caught the hard eyes of Bert for a moment and nodded. Bert knew what he meant. One word from him would have seen Bytheway beaten too. Strangely he responded in kind, giving a civil nod in return. A moment later Bytheway was gone: down the rickety stairs, and out.

Out in the street a fresh wind was blowing. In the pub it had been rank but here the air was fresher. It was spring now and the night was some way off, but Bytheway insisted upon escorting Annie home. In the event they compromised, and Bytheway walked her to The Woolpack, near the bottom of the High Street, from where, she told him, she would go home by cab . Just for a moment she looked at him, into his grey, diffident eyes, and smiled, the kind of smile that lit her eyes and winked and glowed like coals piled in the grate. It was the sort of smile that Bytheway might have warmed his hands by, and he stared at her as though he had forgotten where he was.

'Come along, George,' she said at last, just for a moment or so slipping her arm through his.

'I must see you again,' he said.

This statement, urgent as it was, desperate almost, seemed to move her, but she shook her head.

'I must see you again,' he repeated.

'Write to me,' she said at last. 'Write to me at The Woolpack.'

And so it was that what had begun wretchedly ended wonderfully. With Woodhouse dragging behind him like a ghost in chains, Bytheway led the way down the hill and, troubled as he was by his descent into crime, by the small voice inside him that whispered of his faith, by his grief for Carney and his chafing guilt, and by Deacon, who was acting strangely and perhaps suspected something, he wondered briefly if he had ever been happier.

Chapter Eighteen

Before Woodhouse's tears were dry upon the pub's boarded floor, while the cockfighting was still raging, someone else called there. Brisker suddenly stood among them, though no one saw him come, as if he were some sort of apparition. Ghosts, one may suppose, do not mind bad smells, but Brisker looked as if he had entered a midden. Just like Bytheway and Woodhouse before him, he looked out of place. He wore a top hat with straight sides, a waistcoat, fashionably checked wool trousers and glossy shoes, square-toed. This was a man of money, one who did not belong there. As Woodhouse and Bytheway before him, he began to attract attention, but he did not seem to care. He did not mind whose eyes he caught. Even with his top hat he looked short, but he was angry, and as he stared about him even one or two hardened characters looked away. Eventually Brisker caught hold of a barmaid's arm.

'Albert. Is he here? Is he? Tell him I want to see him. Go to it, madam. Tell him that Mr Brisker wants to see him.'

Upstairs the cock fighting was exciting. Gore and blood and feathers from a savage encounter littered the ring. The crowd was raucous and money was changing hands. Bert did not wish to be disturbed. "E bloody wud cum now!' For a moment he chuntered, but none the less trudged downstairs. He also offered a modicum of respect to his visitor: he drew his mouth into a straight line and glowered, but said something polite after his fashion. Brisker did not care. He looked about him, then drew Bert away. In a corner, he almost pressed himself against the sweaty, stubbly publican.

'Has she been here? Has she?'

"Er 'as.'Bert withdrew a little. One might have thought that the glossy gentleman was the malodorous one.

'Huh, huh,' grunted Brisker, bobbing about. 'Huh, huh. Was she with someone? Was she? Was she? Was she?'

"Er was.'

'Yes, yes,' spluttered Brisker.

'Two gents. Wun a kid. We gid 'im a bit o' a slappin'. Floss wus wi' 'im, any 'ow. Yower wife wus wid a gent, grey 'aired, 'bout six foot. Bytheway wus 'is name. Ah 'eard wun o' 'em call 'im George.'

'George Bytheway,' said Brisker, repeating the name to himself several times. 'George Bytheway. George Bytheway.' Brisker was no longer aware of his companion, and as he repeated the name a light flickered in his eyes, like the guttering of a candle placed in a window to remember the dead.

'I'll kill him,' said Brisker.

Albert did not seem unduly bothered whether Brisker made good this threat or not. Albert wanted to return upstairs but Brisker put a hand on his wrist. It was not wise to touch Albert but, once more, Brisker seemed oblivious to danger. He had something more to say and so detained him. Albert waited while Brisker became more collected. In fact, Brisker underwent a transformation. The wildness left his eyes but, in place of it, a sort of caddish mischief replaced it. Just for a moment Brisker and Albert chortled together, savouring something unsaid, bouncing it back and forth between their eyes.

'Your friend ... you'll let me know if he has any untried girls available? I do so prefer them raw. I must be careful of my wife's health too: a man wants an heir, you know? You understand me?'

'Aw do.'

'But if,' said Brisker suddenly, changing tack, 'if Mrs Brisker comes here again send word to me. If I am at home I'll come immediately.'

A note passed hands between them and Bert nodded. Brisker slipped out into the gathering night like an apparition, there one moment and gone the next.

Chapter Nineteen

Annie had begun to resist her husband, whose abuse of her had worsened. She opposed him in everything, although she was lonely, which made her stance more difficult. Annie was a pariah because she had 'fallen', in other words she had betrayed Brisker. In fact, the rumour which had ruined her was false but no matter; no matter what Brisker did outside the marital bed.

It was fortunate that polite society knew nothing of Annie the prostitute, but it did know that she liked alcohol. She was a 'shocking woman', but Brisker defied opinion of his wife. Although he raged at home he defended her doggedly.

Such was the background of George's Miss Brown, and now poor George had begun to court her. So it was that he and Annie were out one evening. Their forward motion and the trit-trot of their horse were pleasing in themselves, but somewhere outside Stonnall Bytheway pulled the trap over to the verge. Annie waited for his help, but when he was delayed in helping her get down began to do so herself. Terribly apologetic, he raced round and so came upon her momentarily showing her undergarments. He was shocked, turned red and pretended not to notice.

'You're a silly goose,' she said.

He knew what she meant. Bytheway had a little smile at himself and, fleetingly, put his gloved hand over hers ... but he forgot himself. As though she had electrified him he removed his hand.

'You're a goose,' she repeated. None the less, this respect for her, unaware as he was, endeared him to her. For a moment she looked at him, turning over all the nooks and crannies and hidey-holes (she thought) inside him, and smiled. She smiled all the more too when she saw how he looked at her, as though he had forgotten what day it was or how they had got there, but as she thought a little more she seemed saddened by it. They walked on, before sitting down at the side of a field on a blanket that Bytheway had brought.

'George ... You know that I'm married, don't you?' Bytheway sprang up like a jack-in-the-box. Annie shook her head, and lightly touched the blanket beside her, inviting him to sit. 'You'll annoy me if you are going to be stuffy! My husband is away, always away, either on business or upon mischief, I suspect.'

Bytheway was appalled. To be out with an unchaperoned married woman! Criminal conversation! The stuff of scandal, of divorce petitions, of social ruin for her.

'Mr Bytheway.' She used his formal title, as suddenly he appeared so distant. 'I'm already ruined. Untrue rumour had me guilty of an impropriety, and since that time my friends have turned their backs on me. I suspect my husband of having an appetite for prostitutes, but he is not censored.'

'Indeed, but ...'

'What of *his* moral conduct? He might infect me with venereal disease. Never mind the humiliation, or the betrayal. Yet while he is about this mischief I'm commanded not to leave the house. If I do I'm denounced by my neighbours. All this is monstrous! One might naturally suppose that I'd be able to seek reparation in law.'

'And have you?'

'No. I may divorce my husband only if he augments his infidelity with incest, sodomy, bestiality, physical cruelty or desertion. More than this, as we are married he has absorbed me, taken possession of my estate. I have not the means to fund an action against him.'

'You must protest,' said Bytheway. 'You must write to your Member of Parliament.'

'I'm not even able to vote. Have you any conception how unjust that is? I flatter myself that I am the equal of my husband in intellect, and yet have not intelligence enough, it seems, to be entrusted with the franchise. There.' She let out a great puff of air, turned to Bytheway and smiled. 'Am I not indeed a scandalous woman?'

Bytheway was listening gravely, and Annie was grateful for his attention.

'I've not finished yet,' she said. 'Do you know that a woman who is driven into another man's arms by the conduct of her husband will be denied custody of, or even access to, her children? And what of the professions? These are denied to women for want of higher education. Even in our dress we're tortured. We are to have a shape decreed by men, no doubt, and thus we're obliged to wear corsets that constrict us, make us constipated or faint, deform our organs and curve our spine, for fashion. For men! Did you know?'

'Enough!' Bytheway laughed. 'I think I understand you very well.'

'Do you?' She pursed her lips and looked severe.

'Yes, I do, and I'm shocked. I'd never before thought of it. You make me quite ashamed.'

'Good – because so you ought. But you may not be quite as wicked as the rest of your kind.'

'I may be,' said Bytheway, with half a smile.

They stood up and looked about them. To the west Castle Hill heaved up, wooded and green, but at this distance, in this light, it was not distinct but somehow dreamy, like the memory of a hill from childhood. Bytheway recalled the fort on the hilltop. Had the people who had lived there once fought the Romans in these fields, he wondered? Nearby a copse grew along the lane. Amid the trees one green jostled with another, and all the birds of Staffordshire sang. On the other side, over the hedges and over the varying crops, was the tower of Shenstone church, two miles away. Like the hill it lacked clarity, and had a blue tinge. The spires of Lichfield Cathedral also made an appearance, barely visible, like the tips of a rabbit's ears, and nearer at hand there was a high, handsome brown brick house at Wall.

Suddenly Bytheway raised a hand. 'Look!' He pointed and a bird flew past, so close that they flinched. Suddenly, round and about, no more than twenty feet in the air, a group of swallows wheeled and turned and flitted, jinking and swooping. 'How I love swallows! One almost pities the people who've lost them. Except they've come to us!'

Annie was used to rude couplings with her husband. She was unaccustomed to a man whose eyes moistened to see swallows.

'And these flowers,' said Bytheway. 'The daisies and buttercups are all come again.' He turned to her and she looked into his eyes, which were lit from within. Annie thought that he was brimming with sensibility, but in truth he was thinking about the bank. It troubled him so much, and he wanted to tell her. Somehow he felt that with the strange power she had over him she might expiate his offence. He gazed at her. 'All is wonder on an evening like this. How may one not think of the Almighty at such a time?'

'I feel it too,' she said. 'Has your faith returned to you?'

'No.' Bytheway shook his head. 'But by some means it calls to me. Have you ever lain awake and heard someone shouting in the night but been unable to place them or distinguish what they say? So it is with me.' He glanced up again. 'The strangest thing is that I hear the voice which calls to me in you.'

Annie coloured a little. 'I'm a bad woman; I told you that.'

'No. Promise me, promise me that if you should leave him you will come to me.'

Annie looked at him, into him, but said nothing and got to her feet, her chin down, still thoughtful. Bytheway noticed that her eyes were watering. 'Come,' she said. 'We must return.' She offered him her arm and he took it. Together they passed along the lane, with Annie's dress scuffing dust into the air behind her, arm in arm as if they were a wedding day couple.

Chapter Twenty

Late one afternoon Woodhouse and Bytheway were at work in the bank. The bank had closed to customers for the day, and the two clerks sat scratching at their ledgers. Suddenly something rattled in the door. Only Deacon had a key and in he came. What was this? Was the man drunk? They jumped up and bowed, but Deacon did not reciprocate.

By and by they rose, but Deacon still said nothing. Bytheway glanced at Woodhouse and Woodhouse glanced at him. The moment drew out, then Deacon took a step to the left and a step to the right.

'Are you ill, sir?' said Bytheway.

Still Deacon said nothing. Even a glance at the man, too, was enough to confuse them. He seemed to have pushed through a hedge or fought for his life. Still he was mute. The silence which surrounded him extended but, finally, he said something. 'Mr Woodhouse, go! I must speak to Mr Bytheway.'

Woodhouse dared not refuse, but lingered, and wondered if they had been discovered. Perhaps Deacon wanted Bytheway to resign, refund the money and avoid scandal. In that case, would he, Woodhouse, be sacrificed? He glanced at Bytheway and oh, how Bytheway annoyed him! Bytheway's brows were like viaduct arches, his eyes like tunnels. He might have driven a locomotive into his mouth. By every power at his disposal, without speaking, Woodhouse urged Bytheway to be reticent. 'He may not know; he may not know; keep silent!' Woodhouse thought. Heavens above, they worked alongside each other for fifty hours a week: surely Bytheway would take his meaning.

'Quick, man!'

Woodhouse was at last in motion and moved to the door, but his eyes remained on Bytheway. All the time Bytheway looked as if he might spew everywhere at any moment.

'Come back in ten minutes; that will be time enough ... Mr Woodhouse.' Woodhouse stopped. 'You need not listen with your ear to the panel.' Woodhouse coloured; the words had stung him, but he let himself out and closed the door. Deacon watched him walk away toward the market-place. He continued to watch until there was no doubt that Woodhouse had gone, then turned back. Bytheway waited; his finger ends, which he rested on his desk, wobbled with the tension in him.

'George.' Deacon seemed to swallow on something. 'I am deeply troubled. Had I not the right to expect better of you, I who have been as a father to you? I've placed the highest trust in you and yet how did you repay me?'

He dropped his head and shook it slowly. 'Why you, George, why you of all people?' The moment drew out. 'You robbed me. You stole my very sanity. When you said that the Almighty had some purpose in taking my family, do you know how you tortured me? You and your religious consolation! You annoyed me so much that I did not know myself. You must have wondered why I, the best of employers, the most liberal of men, a gentleman, could sometimes so forget himself? Well, you have tortured me with your religious cant.'

So this was it, another assault upon religion! Bytheway almost sank onto the table in front of him. The sigh which escaped him was like the ripple of a wind through the trees. There was a moment of silence between them, then something happened. Suddenly Deacon's voice took on a note which demanded attention. Bytheway waited, listening like someone in bed at night who hears a creak on the stairs.

'I'll tell you my secret, George. You know,' said Deacon, 'when you disputed Darwin, I couldn't bear it. I couldn't bear to hear you. I know how cruel the world is. There's no consolation, no Providence, nothing mapped out for us, only cause and effect. We stand by our actions, we have free will, as you would call it. Well, I blame no one but myself for my misfortunes, I own my responsibility. My wife, whom you knew, died because of me. Not only did I lose Mary, however: I lost our children too, one after another. One after another my children died and, finally, my wife: I had given her the great pox and she died of it, and our children. Syphilis. I gave them syphilis and they died of it.'

Like a great glittering chandelier which dropped from its housings and smashed into a thousand pieces, this disclosure was shattering. This was a revelation which required a moment's thought. Heaven knows, the pox was common enough, but that Deacon should have it! Mr Deacon, richest man in Lichfield, overseer of the workhouse, chairman of this committee, member of that, benefactor, businessman, trustee and pillar of the community.

'Sir!' said Bytheway. Deacon screwed his face up like a paper bag; his lips seemed to turn inside out. 'So,' said Deacon, 'do not dispute Mr Darwin with me. I tell you,' he took in a great draught of air, 'who is the true Lord of Creation? Not the Almighty, George, and not Mr Darwin either, nor his like, but Mr Pox, Mr Syphilis. He decides who shall live and who shall die!'

Deacon's lips now seemed to twist, his face crumpled. Bytheway did not know what to do. 'Hur-hur-hur-hur,' sobbed Deacon.

'Come,' said Bytheway. 'Come, sir, come.' He dragged a chair, scraping, across the slabbed floor and Deacon dropped onto it.

'Hurr-hurr-hurr, hurr.' Bytheway put a hand on Deacon's shoulder.

'You've had a grievous blow,' said Bytheway quietly. ' A grievous blow; and these things are not readily got over.'

'I haven't the faith that you have,' muttered Deacon from his slippy lips. 'If only I had the consolation of faith!'

'No,' said Bytheway. 'At the least,' he said, 'they don't know that they are dead. No suffering can touch them now and you must try to forgive yourself. And seek for hope,' he added, 'as must we all.' Thereafter Bytheway, like a man waiting for an omnibus, continued to stand by Deacon.

Suddenly Woodhouse entered.

'Get out!'

Poor Woodhouse was astonished.

'Get out!'

He paused only to look at Deacon, with eyes like soup plates, then turned on his heels.

The sobbing slowed, became a snuffling and eventually stopped. After a minute or so more, Deacon got up.

'The illness is in abeyance at the moment. Latent. I've had some treatment. I don't know how efficacious it may be in the long term. It seems that it may be years before it returns to me. I have told you this because I needed to tell somebody and, do you know, I had no one to tell, no one. You are such a decent fellow, George, and I had to tell someone. I've wronged you and I'm sorry. I sometimes think that you are the only friend I have, the nearest thing to a friend at least.'

Deacon got up, his ruff of hair under his chops wet, like that of a caterwauling cat doused from a chamber pot. He looked into Bytheway's face, then slouched off to the door, as if the weight of every sin there had ever been weighed upon him. Just before he left he turned back. 'There's something else, George; I may as well tell you. Keep it to yourself, though, not a word! I may sell the bank because of my illness; I haven't decided yet but I may do so. Do not concern yourself; I would provide for you and even for young Woodhouse. One thing: is everything in order? The books would have to be examined, even to the last farthing, but I needn't tell you that:

you know it very well. Is everything well with the bank, George?'

Bytheway nodded.

'Good fellow.'

The door closed upon Deacon, and soon Woodhouse was back, demanding to be told everything. He was incredulous at seeing Deacon in tears, but the possibility of an audit took his mind from Deacon. In fact, hardly anything else was said between them and, in a stunned silence, they eventually completed their work and shut the door upon the bank, rather as a cell door must close upon a prisoner or an animal locked in a cage.

Chapter Twenty-One

Annie and Bytheway were out again during Brisker's absence and, as before, they had turned into Stonnall. Beside the road was a hill with a tree on top and a ring of trees below it. This grove was enticing and they meant to walk up to it.

Annie wore a walking skirt, which she gathered clear of the ground, revealing something of her petticoats. Slyly she cast a glance at Bytheway: had he noticed? He looked to his left, to his right, straight ahead, and he talked without interruption: yes, he had noticed! Suddenly she started laughing. He coloured a little as she teased him, but then he smiled. For a moment he pulled her close, their shoulders bumped, and then he stepped away.

'Oh, George. What will become of us?'

When they passed into the field they realised that they could not surmount the hill without trampling crops, and so they stopped. In any event they had reached a position which was open to the sun. They looked about them and noticed some weeds, growing in the uncultivated strip. These would have been uprooted as worthless, but they were beautiful. The colours jangled with one another.

'Are they flowers or are they weeds?' said Bytheway. 'For they're all the same to me.'

'Let them have their time,' she said, when Bytheway offered to pick them.

In being there together, they each felt a sense of release. Away from Lichfield and Walsall, they were free. They felt as pit ponies must do when brought up to the daylight. The hillside was theirs and no one else's. They felt as if they presided over everything. From left to right was the road. It dipped down with a few houses and farm buildings along it. To the west was Castle Hill. It heaved up, wooded and green, with a high-shouldered farmhouse at the bottom, painted white. On the hilltop were banks and ditches, still visible, which predated the time of Christ.

It seemed that they were alone: the whole world had emptied and been left to them. If only they had known they were encircled in the lens of a spy glass. Someone watched them. In fact, someone had watched them for some while. Bytheway had been so careful, too.

It was a shame because there was such a sense of two-in-oneness between them, such a feeling of peace, perfect concord. Neither one touched the other, there was decorum in all they did, but they were happy. Neither one was used to happiness but, somehow, happiness had stolen upon them, like the man who watched them. No longer shy, Bytheway looked at Annie, who stood narrowing her eyes against the light. The sunlight was so bright that he could see flecks of colour about her irises, and then her eyes smiled for him. In that moment he decided to tell her something. Oh, how the truth will out, but he had to tell her. Somehow he had to tell her about the bank. Somehow he felt that she would have power to set all to rights. He felt that she might expiate his sin; he thought that she would understand, and so he told her.

'Did you know,' he said, putting down his chin, 'that I'm a thief?'

'George?'

'I'm a thief,' he said.

Bytheway would remember her silence later when he thought of this moment. She heard him as if she did not believe him. The silence began to stretch out. As he watched her she turned red. Her fine eyes, which had been warm, became cold. Worse than cold, Annie became distant. She took on that flinty look which he had seen in the pub. Bytheway turned to her and started speaking quickly as he thought that she might walk off.

'Deacon, Mr Deacon, angered me so much. My faith meant everything to me and I've been robbed of it by Deacon, among others: Darwin, Lyell and the rest. But Deacon made it his business to rob me of it and I decided to punish him. I've lost my way, Annie. I'm sorry for it.'

She came up to him and when he put his chin down she forced him to look at her. 'Have you profited from this? Then pay him back. Return the money which you have stolen.'

'Woodhouse is in league with me.'

'Then force Mr Woodhouse to do a similar thing. Force him. How can you ever find your faith by becoming a thief? You've a moral compass, George, and you must find it.' She put her hands on his shoulders. 'George, you have innate decency. That is the man I know. Among all the materialism, the hypocrisy, cynicism and pride all about us you, you are better than that,' she said. Her eyes took on a watery sincerity which twisted Bytheway's guts. 'Now,' she said, 'I desire you to take me home and I must ask you not to seek me out or write to me or contact me by any means until you have set this matter to rights. Oh,' she put her hands to her face, 'what am I saying? What future can there for this improper connection between us? I'm married, Mr Bytheway, and you, perhaps, are not the man I thought you were.' There came a little catch in her voice. 'It may be best that we don't see each again.'

She left her eyes on him and her meaning sank in. The shock made him mute. A minute before she had been warm and now he did not know her, nor she him. He realised something now. To be debarred from seeing her would be unbearable, and yet what happiness could they share? Even if he reformed she would not see him. If he changed she would not know it. He would leave her in Walsall and the gap between them would grow every moment, until he was gone and, eventually, forgotten.

He looked at her and did not hide that he considered her. He was angry. He was exactly the man whom she had believed him to be and her doubting it exasperated him. He was that man, but what was Brisker, the man to whom she returned? Amazingly, he found himself despising 'respectability' – sham respectability, at least – and sham marriages. He had always thought that marriages were God-given, but doubted it now.

' He's violated his marriage vows,' said Bytheway, 'Repudiated them, cancelled them. They're void. You owe him nothing.'

'Yes, perhaps, and I'm heartily sick of him, but he's not a thief, I believe.'

Bytheway sank: from five feet eleven to knee-high nothing in an instant, or so he felt. He could not look at her; he could barely open his eyes.

'Oh, Mr Bytheway, I thought that you were better than this. Do you know, every man I've ever known has failed me. My father betrothed me to my husband, against my wishes, because he felt that Mr Brisker was rich. My father! Is that not pimping? Am I an article of disposable property?And then Mr Brisker himself, who treats me as a brood mare, force-feeds me, imprisons me, betrays me with prostitutes. I might go on. I believed in you, George, and yet you're a thief.'

Annie shook her head and plainly struggled to believe what had been said between them.

'I'll reform,' said Bytheway. 'I'll redeem myself. You may never know it but I shall redeem myself.'

His back seemed to snap up straight, like a scarecrow pillioned by a stake. Annie's size seven boot had jolted his moral compass and set it working. She had not finished yet, either.

'I, too, almost lost my way, as you know,' she said. 'I'm not proud of it. What took possession of me? However, I retreated from it, and so must you. I desire to go home now.'

Annie marched off across the field. This time she did not lift her skirts but ploughed on across the track, sweeping dust into the air behind her. Bytheway scampered in her wake.

When they got to the end of the track, just before they returned to the road, Annie put her hands on his shoulders. This time she said nothing. She fixed him with her eyes and had no need to say more. She did not need his help to get into the trap either, but took her seat and waited to go.

'Men,' she said, once Bytheway was seated. 'I sometimes think that there's not one good one among you.'

Bytheway did not know what to say to that. He slapped the reins across the back of the horse and they went. And so the road between them and Walsall dwindled; the road behind them increased. From here to there and onwards they retraced their steps, and little else was said between them. It was a deflated and soured return journey. There was irony, too, in this: the unknown man who watched them, who was so angry to see them together, had actually witnessed their breach. He lay in the field and cursed, picturing this man and Annie in their intimacy; imagining their laughter at his expense. When Annie laid hands on this man he had wanted to rave, notwithstanding that he had betrayed her only that morning and with a girl too, hardly more than a child. The sense of his outrage made his breathing quick and there was a white light in his eyes, like a carriage lamp seen from afar in the night. His self pity in this moment was an extraordinary thing. 'Cuckold, cuckold, cuckold,' he said repeatedly. 'Me!'

He lay on the ground in country clothing and in a pocket he had a notebook. Frantically Brisker made notes about Bytheway, scribbling, holding up his field glasses in one hand. He might have spared himself the trouble. He would remember every line of Bytheway's face. The question he asked himself was should he pay Albert to punish this man or should he punish him himself? Brisker sucked on this thought as if enjoying a sweet and decided to dole out the recrimination himself. Firstly, he would deal with Annie, who had betrayed him. How could she deceive him when she owed everything to him? Then Brisker slammed his bunched fist into the turf at the thought of Bytheway. He repeated this act of temper again and again. As he punched the ground the wind whistled through him; he sounded like a dog straining against a harness. The dull light in his eyes was more of an animal, too, than of a man, but he was collected, despite his anger, and he would not act now. At a time and place of his choosing they would meet again and soon: somewhere where the lamps burned low or in a dark lane they would have their coming together.

Chapter Twenty-Two

At the earliest opportunity Bytheway spoke to Woodhouse about giving up their theft. All day he waited his moment, and at last he went to the door and locked it. Woodhouse looked up from his work, curious. 'What have you got to say to me, George?' his face seemed to say.

'I cannot continue to steal from the bank, Woodhouse.' Bytheway looked straight into the clerk's eyes.

As ever the clock tick-tocked, tick-tocked. Light poured in from the day outside. The grain of the counter showed in the sunlight. Bytheway seemed to grind something under his shoe. The room itself seemed to wait for Woodhouse's answer.

His reply was not verbal, but anyone would have understood it. It might also have been read very accurately in Bytheway, who put his hands up and sighed. Once he might have been discouraged, but not now. Resolutely, he began to explain himself, his explanation embodying the moderation, probity, sense and rectitude that Woodhouse so much despised. 'Mr Deacon may sell the bank. If he sells the bank we'll be audited, and then we must be caught.'

'Well then,' said Woodhouse. 'What have we to lose in carrying on? I intend to steal up until the last moment. Only with the auditors breathing down my neck will I run for it.'

'No,' said Bytheway. 'We must give it up.' But then an idea presented itself to him. 'Perhaps we may have no need to run. Perhaps we might find someone to forge the stolen notes. I still have the numbers. If the notes were well done, and suitably distressed, perhaps they might be convincing.'

'And who would do it?' asked Woodhouse. ' I can see our advertisement now in the *Lichfield Mercury*: "Forger required: Apply to J.W. Deacon, Bankers of Lichfield. Discretion Essential." Or do you want me to return to that pub? You cannot expect me to ask that brute Albert for a recommendation.'

Bytheway let out a long puff of air. Woodhouse was right: how on earth could they find a forger? 'However,' he said, 'whether or not the bank is sold we must stop now. Think of this: if our theft is discovered confidence would evaporate, and there'd be a run on the bank.' He fanned his hands and his voice took on a 'Look here, old man' note.

Woodhouse yawned.

'The bank', continued Bytheway, 'would be ruined and so, too, would Mr Deacon. All those people whose money is lodged with us would have their accounts frozen; they would have to borrow money to live or to function in their business affairs. We would cause worry at the least and suffering like as not; customers might lose all they have. All they have! We cannot go on hazarding the bank's affairs. I will not. I cannot.'

'Yes, yes,' said Woodhouse. 'But what of me?' He showed the palms of both hands and opened his eyes wide. 'Never mind the old women and their sixpences; what of me? I have been your partner in all of this. Are my views not to be considered?'

'No,' said Bytheway. Had Woodhouse listened to a word? He rubbed a hand across his brow and sighed. 'Your views count for nothing because, I think, you mean to go on.'

'I do!' declared Woodhouse.

'Then I must ignore you.' Bytheway came close to

Woodhouse and framed his words with his hands. 'I know you care nothing for the right and the wrongs of the matter, but think of this. I believe that we'll be caught if we go on, but if we stop now we may cover our tracks. I will do everything in my power to prevent our dishonesty ever coming to light. With good fortune it may never be found, never. You'll have no more access to the cancelled notes. I, and I alone, shall delete them, and no more of them shall be made available to you.'

Woodhouse looked as if he had been asked for his life savings; as if Bytheway wanted him to work for nothing; as if he had been asked to pay the bank for the honour of working there. 'I haven't got enough money for my new life,' he exclaimed.

'Then you must earn it.' Bytheway became busy, and indicated that he had nothing further to add. Suddenly Woodhouse swept some papers onto the floor, knocked a pen off the desk, scattered some ink across the slabs and rammed a ledger back into its place on the shelf. 'You've got some backbone have you, George?' He turned for his answer, eyes like pins. 'Has Mrs Brisker made a man of you, eh? A fine strapping woman like that, eh? Did you tumble her, George? Did you? Did you?'

'How dare you!' Even the mention of Annie's name scalded Bytheway. He could not bear even the most incidental recollections of her.

'Uncorked that bottle at last, did you? It's made a man of you!'

'Stop it!'

'What would Mr Brisker say, eh, George? Not a very pleasant fellow, is he? So Mr Deacon says. You might need a bit of the ginger in you if he caught you.'

'Do not presume to mention that lady to me.' Bytheway jumped to his feet. He hardly knew that he had got up, but he stood tall.

Even so, Woodhouse continued to goad him. He, Horace Arthur Woodhouse, was top dog again. What sport was to be had with George; even the mention of Annie tortured him. But Bytheway was vulnerable elsewhere, too. 'Forgive me, George,

I'm being unfair. In fact, I'm indebted to you for your moral example. You almost make me want to seek out the faith myself: I've no objection to Christianity if it permits both embezzlement and adultery. I'd no idea that it was so congenial.'

'Damn you, sir!'

Bytheway was in motion before he had another conscious thought. Woodhouse jumped up and prepared for him, conscious of his youth and size compared with this smaller, older man, but Bytheway stopped.

'Don't forget, Mr Woodhouse,' said Bytheway, dropping back onto his seat, 'that my name is Mr Bytheway, Mr Bytheway! Do you understand me?' He would not pit himself against his clerk's youth and strength but would beat him with quiet authority instead. In that instant Woodhouse's advantage ended. This time a ledger was thrown across the floor. More papers followed the ledger and another pen bounced upon the slabs.

'I'll not be put me in my place like this, George. I shall not!' Woodhouse shouted, but this time his face was crumpled, like a boy who had been refused more pudding. 'I've a hold over you, George. Do you understand me?'

Bytheway turned his eyes on Woodhouse without emotion. He looked immaculate, as he had at the start of the day: short haired, clean-shaven, buttoned up and neat, whereas Woodhouse looked like an unruly pupil in a school for rough boys. 'Keep to your work, Mr Woodhouse, and be grateful for what you have. Aspire to be something better than a thief or a felon. Be sure to make up your ledger before you leave and clean up this debris from the floor, including the ink. I'm going for the night now. Goodnight, Mr Woodhouse.' Bytheway bowed with great courtesy and, with only a hint of a irony, left. The door closed behind him softly: there was no occasion for upset, it seemed to suggest; the matter was settled.

'Confound the man!' shouted Woodhouse at the blank, impassive door. Curses followed, with slammings and throwings and stompings round about the room. At last, however, he settled over his work as a hawk may crouch over a kill while it rips the guts out of something. All the time he bunched and unbunched his face, his eyes opening wide, mad wide, then becoming slits. Poor Horace! Poor Horace! He burned with a sense of injustice: how dare Bytheway show him such a lack of consideration! In his heart, too, he felt Bert's fists upon him, and remembered how Floss had abandoned him. He blamed Bytheway for that humiliation, too, and even as he sat there and did Bytheway's bidding he was deciding how to avenge himself. Did George Bytheway think that he could better him? He was mistaken. Woodhouse would not rest until he got his revenge, and he thought he knew exactly how to get it.

Chapter Twenty-Three

In the days after his breach with Annie, Bytheway tried to keep himself busy. He was frightened to be alone and unoccupied; he did not wish to think; so he was busy, busy, busy. At work he distracted himself with trips into town, going out to collect money from people who could not come to the bank, or calling to recommend the bank to potential customers. On one such occasion he was in the city, near the market-place, under the statue of Dr Johnson. He chatted for some time to a customer of the bank, not noticing a certain small, black-haired gentleman who stood near them, absorbed, it seemed, by the statue.

That night Bytheway went to The Swan. He sat there for some time reading a newspaper, again not wanting to be alone. The noise of the place and the conversations around him were good for his spirits. The same small, malevolent gentleman sat almost opposite him. Once again Bytheway did not so much as notice him.

It seemed that Brisker had a facility for making himself invisible, but that night Bytheway could not be blamed for failing to spot him. It was a black night, and once Bytheway went to the window. The light was bright behind him and he looked out into the dark. His window looked away from Walsall and Bytheway, who was thinking of Annie, turned so that he faced her. Across the few miles between them she would be passing this night by, and Bytheway tried to picture her, so near but irretrievably lost to him.

He stood in the light in his bedroom window for perhaps a minute and, unknown to him, in the shadows, the same, small malign man watched him. Some light from somewhere found out the white in Brisker's eyes. Had anyone been close they might have heard him, too.

'Huh-huh-huh,' he said. As he said this he slapped the palm of his hand with a weapon, a cosh. 'Huh-huh-huh.'

When Bytheway left the window he drew the curtains, and sometime afterward his light was extinguished. A few minutes later, a shadow moved towards Bytheway's door. From shadow to shadow, dark to dark, Brisker drifted to the door, treading carefully. Stealthily he reached the handle at last and imperceptibly turned it. He pushed ever so gently against the door but it was locked. In his pocket he had a tool to break the lock. He thought for a moment, but then a light came on in the house. It was Bytheway, who had decided to read for a little while, and so it was that Brisker did not strike that evening.

Bytheway drew back the curtains to a fine, bright day. It was a day to encourage anyone, and he felt happier to see it. He had a sense, too, that this would be a special day: he had these intimations sometimes. It was a day to be out, if possible, and, much to Woodhouse's disgust, Bytheway had an errand to make. On such occasions he sometimes carried a lot of cash but, somehow, never thought about being attacked. Indeed, who would attack Mr Bytheway on his rounds? Lichfield was a respectable city.

So, like a good chap, he carried his money bag and returned to the bank. As he went he made recognitions of passers-by and people acknowledged him, too. This pleased him from top to bottom. He was becoming himself again.

Bytheway was elated for another reason, too. He had renounced crime, and had an excuse to contact Annie. He was like a child running home to show his mother something. In his hand to please her he had his promise made good, and he hoped to gratify her if she would but consent to hear him.

As he walked back to the bank he thought so deeply that he failed to see some people who spoke to him, but they smiled at his obvious distraction. Had they known it, however, he thought of Brisker; and how strange a thing that was because Brisker was following him along the road. Once again Brisker trailed him but with no thought to attack him, not in daylight, not in the open; but then Mr Bytheway placed himself in jeopardy.

In St John's Street the railway passed over the road. There was a bridge, flanked by two towers, which spanned the road and carried the railway across it. In each of the towers was a passageway where, with the bridge over and around them, a person was vulnerable. Effectively, except from in front or behind, a pedestrian disappeared from view. It was dark beneath the towers too, and the view one had of another person was restricted. In short, this made the arches perfect for an ambush. For these reasons, as Bytheway approached the bridge, Brisker glanced about him. There was nobody to see him, neither behind nor in front. This was the moment! Brisker felt his breathing quicken, his hand tighten upon his cosh.

Bytheway drew near the bridge, unknowing. Perhaps in his mind he was walking along a bending lane with Annie, or some such. Behind him Brisker had broken into a trot, and the distance between the men dwindled, but then Bytheway stopped. Brisker stopped. Had some sense warned Bytheway? No, he had stopped to admire the bridge! A bridge was a bridge, surely? Brisker was most put out. This was damned inconvenient. However, Bytheway pondered the structure's heraldry. Over the bridge's central span were the arms of England and four other devices, those of the Anson, Bagot, Forster and Dyott families. While Brisker hopped foot to foot, Bytheway next admired the bridge's design. It was built of stone and had, with its battlements and insignia, been designed to look like a great city gateway. It was very imposing: 'Capital!' thought Bytheway. 'Capital!' Indeed, just then a train ran across the bridge, all rumble and thunder and smoke. The smoke drifted down and then Bytheway, thrilled with the train, walked through the archway.

The first Bytheway knew of Brisker was when he heard footsteps. Bytheway imagined that someone was in a fearful hurry and politely began to step aside. He turned and saw a nasty little man with nasty narrow eyes come running up. The man produced a cosh, and took Bytheway by the throat. Bytheway slammed back into the hard stone wall.

'Make a cuckold of me, sir! Me!' said the man.

Part dumbfounded, part frightened, part amazed, realisation dawned on Bytheway who this man must be. The shock of being manhandled, strangled, unmanned him. He had some instinct to fall back upon his manners. 'I'm sorry, sir, but I really must protest.' It was the voice which he used in the bank to disgruntled customers.

Suddenly Brisker's fist bounced off Bytheway's jaw. Bytheway began to say something else. He would have said more but the cosh caught him a glancing blow. He made a sort of animal sound now. It surprised him, especially as it resounded along the tunnel. Suddenly Bytheway had a moment of terror: his manners were useless. This man would kill him, here under the bridge! Spurred on, he defended himself, ramming his fist into the side of Brisker's face. The little man fell back and Bytheway pushed him to the opposite wall There was a whir of fists between them, boots scratching on the gravel, and one caught the smell of the other. With a hooked hand Bytheway scrabbled for Brisker's eyes, but Brisker caught him at the wrist and bounced the cosh off his eggshell head. Somehow, now, the fight took on a different character for Bytheway. Somehow, too, his body and mind had grown disconnected. He wound down like a clockwork toy, which terrified him, because how would he defend himself? Brisker struck him again, and Bytheway knew that he was beaten. Brisker struck him again, and Bytheway knew little more; though perhaps, truth to tell, he remembered something. A little medley of reminiscences came to him later: falling, the ground rushing at him, Brisker's feet, and a view of the pavement, down at ground level, then darkness.

The darkness was kind to Bytheway. To have been conscious throughout what happened next would have been awful. Brisker stood over Bytheway and howled. He put back his head and bellowed. The noise reverberated along the archway; and it was this sound of visceral triumph which attracted someone.

Even now Brisker had not yet finished. Even after he was disturbed he kicked Bytheway, so hard that his opponent, inert and heavy, shifted on the ground, and then Brisker kicked him again. The person who interrupted him, a elderly man, shouted and even came on. Brisker beckoned him. Hiding his face, Brisker made a inviting gesture with one hand. What happened next was a strange thing, too. The pensioner became the focus of those mad eyes and Brisker showed his teeth. The almsman stopped. For a moment more the old man and Brisker looked at one another. In that instant they were the only two, it seemed, in the whole city of Lichfield; and then Brisker, still seeking to hide his face, turned and bounded off, like a fiend in the sort of dream which wakes us in the night.

Chapter Twenty-Four

The man who had disturbed Brisker knew better than to chase him far. He quickly returned to Bytheway, calling for assistance as he went. Still curled up like a hair in the bottom of a bath tub, Mr Bytheway was carried to a nearby house, his head banging against the door frame as he was taken in. He was placed upon a chaise longue, where he lapsed in and out of consciousness while a succession of people leaned over him, patronised him, poked him, swabbed him and bothered him. One of these was the apothecary, Mr Jukes. Jukes told him that he had suffered a nasty knock (an opinion that Bytheway might have endorsed). Next came Mr Deacon, who seemed almost embarrassed; he hardly knew how to express his concern, and gave Bytheway a manly clap upon the shoulder that had been bruised by Brisker's cosh.

The sight of Deacon animated Bytheway. 'I must return. Must return. The earliest opportunity. Tomorrow, Mr Deacon. Tomorrow.'

'Not at all,' said Deacon. 'I'll stand in for you at the bank until you regain your strength. See what mischief you've been up to, eh?'

'No,' said Bytheway, raising up a hand like a puppet drawn by a string. 'No. I'll be back in the morning. Back in the morning.'

'You hear that?' said Deacon. He gave Bytheway another clap on the shoulder and turned to the people standing round: 'What a fellow! What dedication. Splendid! Splendid! No,' he said, speaking very slowly and very loud, 'No, you've had a nas-ty kn-ock. I must stand in for you. It's about time that I attended more closely to the bank.'

'No,' moaned Bytheway. 'Noooo!' He was still protesting when he was removed to his home some while later. He did what he could, but failed to convince anyone that he was fit to work – thereby leaving Deacon free to interfere in the bank's affairs. 'Oh dear! Oh dear,' moaned Bytheway repeatedly. 'Oh dear; oh dear.'

The first hours after the attack were not coherent for Bytheway; once his mind cleared, however, he dreaded discovery, so much so that even the workings of his clock unsettled him. His mind somehow kept pace with its slow tick-tock, and he found that he lived every minute. Worst of all were the quarter, half and hourly chimes. The clock struck after a succession of rattles, which had the effect of a drum roll. With each minute discovery seemed more likely but, once Deacon had insisted upon relieving him, what could Bytheway do? He could only wait to see if the next steps upon the stairs were those of the constable.

Once there was a soft tread on the stairs. He listened to the progress of someone coming slowly upwards. Finally the door opened with a creak: 'I'm so sorry! I did it and regret it all; can you forgive me?' was almost his response to his landlady who asked if he wished for tea.

'Yes, tea, if you please,' he said to be rid of her. 'No, no tea after all. I thank you,' he said, so that she had no reason to come back. How his landlady thought tea might save all the troubles of the world! Not so.

Bytheway lay and slept for a few minutes but woke up shouting. It was no good: there could be no rest, so he sat and considered his predicament. One thing which troubled him was if Brisker were caught and sought to justify himself. Such an occurrence might induce an investigation into Bytheway's conduct at the bank. He had to concede that Brisker was likely to be caught. There had been such a fuss, and the following report had appeared in the local press.

Heroic Bank Clerk Frustrates Robber

On the 13th day of this month Mr. George Bytheway, senior clerk of the Lichfield Bank of J.W. Deacon, was attacked as he carried funds from a customer to the bank. Mr. Bytheway carried almost £100, and only his spirited defence of the money in his care frustrated the design of his assailant. So courageous was Mr. Bytheway in defending his burden that the assailant was obliged to strike him more than once, with a cosh or other such implement, which rendered Mr. Bytheway insensible. The miscreant, once disturbed, was obliged to leave the scene without the money, which Mr. Bytheway, even in insensibility, clutched to his bosom, and escaped on foot along St John Street.

After the incident Mr. Bytheway was carried into a nearby house, where he was attended by an apothecary. Mr. Deacon was also quick to succour him and made haste to praise his employee, saying that he and his staff would stop at nothing to protect the bank and the interests of its customers. Indeed, Mr. Bytheway, even as he was carried away, insisted that he would return to the bank on the following morning and wanted 'no fuss', an injunction he made repeatedly. Mr. Deacon said that this devotion to duty proved Mr. Bytheway's moral character and promised him a substantial reward once he returns to work which, thankfully, by the blessing of Providence, is not expected to be long in coming.

Mr. Hardupp, of the Lichfield Constabulary, said that no stone would be left unturned in the hunt for the attacker and, in due course, once their artist returned from a short holiday in Broadstairs, a poster would be circulated making known the man's description. In his delirium Mr. Bytheway described the man as seven feet tall, with an eye patch, but it is thought, in fact, that the assailant has a small stature, short, glossy, black hair and nasty, narrow eyes, although, in justice, it must be admitted that he was respectable and dressed as a gentleman. Mr. Deacon also offered a substantial reward for the apprehension of the miscreant and said that anyone who hazarded the affairs of the bank would be hunted down and made subject to the harshest strictures of the law.

The *Lichfield Mercury* also added its voice to the praises of Bytheway and called him a 'stout-hearted oak, strong in trunk and branch, rooted in old-fashioned British decency'. It was all too much! Bytheway decided that he must return to work. There followed a vexing set of letters between Bytheway and Deacon. Bytheway begged to return; Deacon refused. Bytheway asked again; Deacon refused. Bytheway asked again and Deacon ignored him. Bytheway asked again and Deacon said 'No'. Bytheway begged, threatening to go to work in his linen, and finally Deacon agreed – but Bytheway must come to work late. Come to work on the next day, if he must, but come late.

So it was, praise be! He would return to work. He would carry on as before, save in so far as Annie was concerned. He would never be as he had been, not without Annie, but he had a wild hope. Perhaps Brisker might divorce Annie? Oh, imagine the joy of that! Bytheway would marry her, if she would have him. He would like that. He feared for her, however, with Brisker. It was also true that any scandal might impair his ability to protect her, but these were problems for another day. Let him be quiet, set his affairs in order and be careful, if he could, not to draw any attention to himself .

The next morning, Bytheway got up early for work. He washed, shaved and dressed as usual, though with some difficulty, and ate a morsel of breakfast. When the time came to leave he stood on his step and looked at the world: no longer the invalid or hero but Mr Ordinary going to work.

The ordinariness of that ordinary day pleased Bytheway hugely that morning. The city was itself, just what it had been before the world turned upside down. No one bothered him; everything was in perfect order. Those people he met were busy with their own lives: some spoke, some did not; he raised his hat to ladies, but kept on. He was nearly there now. Down he went along Breadmarket Street, rounded the corner and there he was confronted with something. He might have known! He might have known! There was a brass band. A brass band! Deacon was waiting for him too, but others besides: there was the Mayor in his robes, Sergeants at Mace, escorting the Mayor, themselves in regalia, various aldermen and a goodly number of citizens. Otherwise there were union flags outside the bank, festooned upon the lamp posts, and children from the workhouse, lined up! Bytheway turned and made off.

'There he is!'

Bytheway turned his back and ran away down Bore Street. He ran like a skylark, dragging a wing, but made a brave attempt. He ran almost to Stowe Street, pursued by aldermen, Deacon, children from the workhouse, two or three newspapermen, several well-wishers, all and sundry, blighters all.

'Swines,' muttered Bytheway. In fact, he struggled when they laid hands on him. Only weight of numbers brought him to the bank. All the way the devils backslapped him, jollied him, linked arms with him and so on, while he wished them all dead. The band struck up again, and when he reached the bank the children sang two songs. Never, never, never had he been more embarrassed.

'What an infernal din,' said Bytheway.

The Mayor and aldermen were a little surprised at this candour. The occasion faltered somewhat for a moment or two. The Mayor considered Bytheway's extraordinary frankness: 'Goodness,' he thought, 'what directness!' However, it was, after all, the truth, so he too began backslapping Bytheway.

In that minute, Bytheway came as close to committing murder as he had done through all the course of his life. Given any opportunity he would have locked himself in the bank. However, like an oven-ready duck, the Mayor waddled forward. Too many civic dinners hindered him, but he made a stately progress. Finally, he bowed to Bytheway, to the crowd and to the dignitaries. There followed a moment of waiting. The Mayor lifted a bony hand, gathered the attention of everyone, and blew it like a kiss toward Bytheway. In fact, the old devil became quite dewy-eyed, and shook his head from side to side in contemplation of the hero. Bytheway wanted to kick the old fart's arse. 'This man,' said the Mayor. 'This son of Lichfield. This fine, decent, manly man.' So the Mayor continued. 'It is no accident that the funds of this Corporation are vested in Mr Deacon's most reputable bank. Children, mark you well a man of true British pluck, a man undaunted by a bully with a cosh, who defended his master's funds almost at the cost of his own life. One might travel far across the boundless tracks of ocean, to the furthest corners of empire, to find another such man; a man whose integrity, decency and attention to duty have been marked these many years; a man worthy of the country and fair city which bore him; a man worthy of emulation in the smallest part of his life. Therefore, in consideration of your high renown in this city, I have the honour to present you, George Bytheway, with a scroll marking your high courage, probity and sense of duty, celebrating you as a true son of Lichfield.'

'Hurrah! Hurrah! Bravo! Good old George! For He's a Jolly Good Fellow ...'

'For He's a Jolly Good Fellow, For He's a Jolly Good Fel-el-ooow' suddenly struck up among the crowd. Woodhouse started it. Like cats they all began to halloo. The band belatedly joined in, the children waved flags, people jostled to see, and someone even asked Bytheway to bless a baby. Suddenly he was drawn forward and presented with a parchment scroll, then Deacon came forward. 'Dear old George.'

Although thoroughly disenchanted, Bytheway watched Deacon. How Deacon loved an audience. He behaved as if the crowd were there to see him. He came up tottering, as if his top hat unbalanced him. Was there any need to fish out his watch? Did he need to parade, as he did, up and down? He looked as if he wanted to sell them something. How strange, thought Bytheway: while he wilted under scrutiny, Deacon appeared bigger. Even his gingery ruff projected under his chin, and he extended his chest so much that he might have toppled. For a moment, indeed, he seemed to forget Bytheway. He stared at him as if he had never seen him before in his life, then grabbed his hand. 'Dear old George.'

This was not a culture in which men were permitted to display overt emotion; none the less, Mr Deacon dabbed at one eye with a handkerchief. Bytheway looked at all the new penny faces of the children. 'No!' he thought, 'Do not look at me so.' He was almost moved, too, to see their attention to Deacon. The children listened to Deacon like sheepdogs trembling for the word of command.

'In consideration', said Deacon, 'of your service to me and my bank over many years and your courage, integrity and honour, you dear old stick, I take great pleasure in presenting you with a token, from my own pocket, of £50. You have well deserved it, George. Give me your hand.' Once again Deacon, flushed and emotional, wrung the life out of George's paw.

'Speech! Speech!'

The cry went up for the hero to spare them a few words from his great soul. The marvel was drawn forward and quiet settled round him. In this silence Woodhouse somehow drew Bytheway's eyes to himself. He tried to communicate with Bytheway. He implored him not to confess. Frankly, he was alarmed that Bytheway, being Bytheway, might divulge everything there and then. The two clerks looked at each other, although who might say what they understood by it? Bytheway stepped forward. 'I thank you all, but am entirely unworthy of the attention which you have bestowed on me. I can say no more.'

'George!'

Just when it seemed that they could think no more of him their admiration grew further. 'Oh, George! What a card! What a dry dog! Oh dear, what a character!' The laughter which followed Bytheway's speech was somewhat hysterical. Bytheway wondered if they even knew what they laughed at, which was certainly the case of the children. Had he blown his nose they would have cheered him, but it was left to the Mayor to point to the moral of the case.

'You see, children? Mark you well the modesty of the true British hero: brave in deed but humble in character.'

The children's eyes grew wider in consideration of this paragon of all the virtues, George Bytheway, then they all snapped to attention. The band struck up the National Anthem, and the Mayor, who had a mistress in a house near there, and Deacon, who had the pox, and Bytheway, grand embezzler, and Woodhouse, who was Woodhouse, sang like blackbirds in the dawn, and the children sang, in their innocence, believing every word of it.

Chapter Twenty-Five

The same day on which he received his award Bytheway sat thinking. Sitting in firelight, he watched the shadows cast by the flames playing around him. Usually they entertained him, but he was not in a mood to be diverted. Tellingly, the light caught in his eyes as he pondered Annie, of whom he had heard nothing. He often sat in this manner, the world of the bank and the busy day contracting to this room, this pool of light, and the thoughts parading through his head. There was nothing better than firelight and solitude to encourage thought.

Bytheway thought so deeply that he did not hear the soft knock on the door. Whoever knocked was obliged to knock again, and at last he jumped up, shocked, and opened it. His housekeeper stood before him. Kindly, old, knowing, she passed him a note that had been brought to the door and he took it, just remembering his manners before he opened it. Forgotten, she left him, and softly closed the door behind her.

Bytheway read the note as though he did not believe it, then read it again, looked at the reverse, and re-read it. Within that minute he had taken his hat and coat, left the room, come back, burned the letter and left again. Down the stairs he went, shutting the outside door with a bang.

His housekeeper watched him from the window, and wondered where he was going in such a hurry. He was rushing so much that he was trying to put on his coat as he walked. She watched as long as she could, then returned to her own pool of candlelight.

In no time at all Bytheway had reached the Cathedral. The spires were beautiful, as always, but he ignored them. Likewise he dismissed Minster Pool, his old favourite; it was lovely, but it went unnoticed. In a similar fashion he was not drawn into conversation by passers-by: with a tip of his hat and a quick word he went on. Before long he reached the Swan Hotel and, after a word with someone and the passing of a coin, went up to a room. Outside the door he radiated pent up energy like a gas mantle. He knocked, and Annie opened the door.

To that moment he had been full of purpose, but now formality, manners, diffidence took possession of him until he noticed a bruise on her face. As he looked at this she pulled a face and waited impassively. She looked tired in her crumpled dress, and her hair was down. A sweep of her hair over one shoulder framed her face and drew attention to her injury. At his own bruising, and his politeness, she gave her head a little shake and her mouth turned up at the corners. He took her hands – guilty, wretched, angry about her bruise – and then she leaned on him. In that moment he felt her weight and warmth, the closeness of her, and hastily pushed the door shut behind him, begrudging every moment that his hand was removed from her body. Her head was on his shoulder now and he could smell her, see the mix of black and brown in her hair. She was his. He dared, as he had never done before, to put his hands on the turn of her hips, so that her flesh gave under his fingertips, then she looked up and turned her mouth to his.

Much as he hated tawdry infidelity, Bytheway began to help her out of her dress, gently, apologetically at first and then frantically, until she stood in her undergarment, which hung upon her breasts, and then she deftly began to undress him. Her fingers were nimble and quick, and she hardly glanced away from his eyes, smiling at his quickened breathing. Then, stepping over their strewn clothes, she led him to her bed.

From that time Bytheway was virtually resident in The Swan until, for safety's sake, he moved Annie to another hotel. This was outside Lichfield but within easy reach: thank heaven for trains! Annie had left her husband because, for the first time, he had been violent toward her. He had been angrier about her meetings with Bytheway than she had ever seen him, and after boasting about leaving his rival unconscious in the gutter he had struck her, knocking her to the ground. Once was enough. Although he had begged her forgiveness she had taken the first opportunity to leave, taking with her a little money, although, heaven knows, it would soon run out. None the less, she had left him, and to prevent Brisker tracing her she had walked a considerable way into Lichfield, carrying a heavy bag.

The period when he saw Annie daily was the happiest time of Bytheway's life. Every day after work they spent the evening together, sometimes going out into the countryside or taking the train to a place where they were not known. On a Saturday evening they sometimes went somewhere more distant and stayed overnight. Bytheway could pretend to be married on these occasions. How proud he was to introduce her as his wife: his heart fluttered inside him. Whenever they were together he felt bigger, taller, better.

How bizarre it was that through her Bytheway found his faith again. Sometimes on a Sunday morning, away from Lichfield, they attended church together. By the most amazing grace he found faith, love and affirmation in this sinful but beautiful and, to him, chaste relationship

Annie, for her part, had also seldom been happier, and although troubled by the thought of Brisker she began to forget him. Bytheway was the very opposite of her husband: he was gentle and attentive; in fact, she was the centre of his world and, as they went on, he grew in confidence. She began to coax so much from him: spontaneity, a sense of humour, and joy. She had stopped drinking spirits and was feeling well, better than she had done for months. She had a bloom about her and her cheeks were shiny and bonny. All in all life was good, and all they had to do was to make sure that their happiness lasted.

Chapter Twenty-Six

A little while into their new lives, Annie and Bytheway were regular worshippers at the church at Burton. It seemed as if they had always belonged there. Of course, they had to explain why they lived apart, but convinced everyone that they were married. Indeed, to see them, walking arm in arm, they looked like newly-weds. Annie would look up at him as she smiled and talked, and he, sometimes pulling her closer, would joke and make sly comments, which he always betrayed by his grey eyes sparkling before he made them.

One Sunday they had shaken the hand of the vicar in the doorway as they, and the others in the congregation, left after church. They sat on a bench at the foot of the tower and watched as the last men in hats and women in bonnets retired along the tree-lined path. Soon afterward the vicar also left, but they remained, sitting hard against the sun-warmed tower. In front of them the path wound to the gate, wandering through uneven ground. In the grass were blooms of different sorts, some weeds but all colourful. There was also a bent old yew tree which had watched the church being built. Everything was so peaceful. There were occasional ripples of birdsong and the sound of flies, the scent of something too, perhaps wet earth after a rainstorm that morning.

As they sat they were untroubled by anyone; Lichfield, Walsall, Brisker, the bank seemed a thousand miles away; they were the only two in the whole world. As the lovers watched a butterfly passed between the gravestones, Annie said that each stone marked not a body but an immortal soul.

'Yes,' said Bytheway. 'Yes!' He turned to share the thought with Annie but she was unable to speak. As he looked at her, to his surprise, she began crying. Annie was very private about this and sought no solace from him. She cried silently, as a child might under the blankets who expected no comfort to come. Bytheway was shocked and put his hand on hers, but she looked away, not wanting to share her thoughts with anyone. He was a little stung, but such was her sense of propriety, it seemed, that she wished to avoid being seen crying publicly, even by him. She was very mindful of propriety just then, what the world would think, because they were so far out on a limb. At last she finished crying and Bytheway cast round for something to say, something cheerful.

'George,' she said.

He stopped. He could tell that she had something important to tell him.

'I think that I may be with child. It is your child, George; not Brisker's but yours.'

Bytheway reached across and put his hand on hers, without saying anything, without looking either. He bent forward and she heard two or three deep gasps come out of him, then a sob, just once. Suddenly they jumped to their feet and he wrapped his arms around her, and she him. They laughed, laughed out loud, hugged, then rocked, shifting their weight, rocking some time, for two, three, five minutes, or more, and at last he looked at her and kissed her. This was the most wonderful news and the most awful; the best and the worst, at one and the same time.

'The bank,' she said. 'They're going to catch you and put you in prison.'

'No,' he said. 'No. I've hidden my tracks as best I can. They may never know.'

'And Brisker,' she interrupted. She looked up at him, her face lined with worry. Bytheway shook his head and sighed. 'And these people,' she said. 'These people who are so kind, once they know, if they know, we'll be cast out. There'll be nowhere to go. I shall not be able to support myself, or our child, if you are in prison. I'll be destitute and the child will be taken from me.'

'No,' he declared. 'No! They shall not find out.'

'I've wanted a child so badly,' she said.

'My child,' he said. 'I'm to be a father.' He said this as if he could not believe it himself.

'Your child,' she whispered. She looked at him for a moment and smiled, her eyes shining. 'An immortal soul,' she said, 'of our making.' And they prayed a moment for their child, that all would end well for him – for Bytheway anticipated that it was a boy – and, briefly, they laughed and hugged again and he cried and she cried a little to see it.

It was impossible to appreciate the flux of emotions in them as they sat and contemplated this news, and for some time they did nothing but think of it. As they sat his hand rested on hers and they were joined by body and soul. Bytheway wished that they might always be joined. He must, must find some way of evading discovery of his crime. He thought again about finding a forger to replicate the stolen notes. There were people who did such things, but how to find them? What of Brisker, though? He knew that Brisker hunted them. What of him? When he knew Annie was pregnant, too, what would he do if he found her? Bytheway dreaded that Brisker would hurt Annie and the child she carried, his child. It was in thinking of Brisker, however, that a thought occurred to Bytheway.

He looked across to Annie, who sat side on to him. She felt him shift and turned to him, a question in her eyes.

'I'll go and see Mr Brisker,' said Bytheway, 'and tell him that you're carrying my child. I'll ask him to behave as a gentleman and set you free. If I must I'll goad him into divorcing you. Your time with Mr Brisker is over; he must be made to see that.'

Annie shook her head. 'He's not a gentleman, George. He may hurt you. It will end badly, George; please do not do so, for my sake.'

'I have to do so, absolutely for your sake!'

Annie put her head down and shed some tears again. This time Bytheway had nothing cheerful to say and sat with his back straight and looked out over the headstones, his left hand holding tightly onto Annie's right hand, which lay dead under his grip.

Chapter Twenty-Seven

One evening after work, Bytheway went by train to Walsall and on from there to Brisker's fine old house. He was purposeful initially but hesitated just outside the property. The place, with its eclectic mix of the old and new, was like a house in a fairy story. He felt that if he passed through the gatehouse the gates would close of their own volition behind him. The house was charming but seemed to lure him, as if there were a monster living inside. He proceeded, however, went to the door and rang the bell. The jangle of the doorbell was musical and attractive, but spoiled because Bytheway could hear his own breathing. He felt that his guts had been twisting ever since he set out, until now he was barely able to breathe.

There was a strange mix of emotions in him as he stood there. He anticipated Brisker every moment but, equally, thought of Annie. Her saw her influence there in everything which was attractive, and he was sure that Brisker must feel similarly. After the second ring a servant came, and Bytheway removed his hat and demanded to see the master. He half hoped that Brisker would be out, but Brisker was not out and the servant asked his name.

'Mr George Bytheway,' he said. The servant asked him to wait and Bytheway was left in the hall, with its attractive tiles in a geometric pattern and a clock with a slow tick-tock, tick-tock. Once again, his heart fluttered but he resisted his nerves; he rehearsed what he would say, and repeated it to himself. He heard footsteps and expected the servant, but it was Brisker.

'You!'

Bytheway made a noise as if he had just plunged into freezing water. There was something about Brisker. He looked at people as if he knew every sin which they had ever committed and despised them for it; so it was now. Bytheway thought of an animal which he had once seen in a gamekeeper's trap. The keeper had had it secure but, given a chance, it would have bitten him to the bone.

'What do you want?' Brisker's top lip rose and Bytheway saw his yellowed teeth. 'As if I did not know?'

'I desire to speak with you, privately.' Bytheway spoke firmly, though perhaps a little reedily.

Brisker made a gesture to a door nearby, and threw it open. Bytheway followed him. Inside were large windows, dark furniture, paintings on almost all the walls and a deep, green carpet, with a contrasting rug lying across the fireplace.

The outline of Brisker presented itself. Perhaps by design he stood with his back to the light.

'I'll not prevaricate,' said Bytheway. His heart bumped and thumped in his chest. He swallowed. 'I've come to ask you to divorce Annie.'

'Damn you, sir!' Brisker stamped over from the window 'No! Does that answer your question?'

'I must ask you to reconsider.'

'How dare you! What have you done with her? Tell me, huh, huh. Tell me!'

'She shall not return to you!' Bytheway was growing loud. 'Your relationship with her ended when you raised your hand to her.'

'You! Shall I raise my hand to you?'

158

'You may try.'

'I've not yet decided,' said Brisker, 'how you shall leave this house. The maid could be persuaded to forget, huh, huh, that she saw you.'

'A man brought me here and is waiting for me outside,' lied Bytheway 'And Annie knows that I've come here.'

Brisker gagged on his disappointment. He looked as if he had swallowed a fly. 'Perhaps I should follow you again,' he suggested. 'Do you know, Mr Bytheway, that I stood outside your room at night and watched as you stood in the window? When you were abed I was without, and even tried your door handle once'

The thought of this inhibited Bytheway from sleeping when he thought of it later, but for the moment he stood tall. Brisker made a creaking noise and mimed the turning of a door handle.

'I'm very wary now, Mr Brisker,' said Bytheway. 'You need not trouble to follow me again. I've also taken precautions against any forced entry into my home.' He hid his fear well but detected a malicious thrill in Brisker, who seemed to realise that he had unsettled him. Bytheway's pride was stung. 'I must tell you too, Mr Brisker, that you've grown too accustomed to intimidating women. You don't frighten me.'

'Oh!' Brisker drew his top lip up and made a sort of chuckle, a musical little chortle; his eyes were lit. It was the kind of elation that recalled an elf in a fairy story, counting his golden pennies in a cottage deep in the woods.

'I must ask you,' repeated Bytheway, 'that you divorce your wife. Not for me, for her. You owe her that, monster as you were to her.'

Like a whip, Brisker's left hand flashed out and caught Bytheway across the cheek. Bytheway, despite every expectation, was shocked. He reeled back, but caught a second blow across an upturned arm. For a moment the men wrestled; just for a moment.

'Villain! Adulterer!' Bytheway flinched as Brisker shouted within a foot of his face. Spittle picked at his face, landed in his eyes, entered his mouth. For a moment he had a view – too close

159

– of every flaw in Brisker's face: he could smell his hair oil, inspect his yellowed teeth, see the stubble growing on the sides of his angular face. Then the men stood apart.

Bytheway watched, trembling. He was a gentleman, however, and a gentleman must behave as a gentleman. Rather inanely, given the circumstances, he tugged his cuffs over his sleeves. Brisker passed to and fro, back and forth, back and forth, but Bytheway decided to play his trump card. His heart thumped against his rib cage. 'I must tell you that Annie is carrying my child.'

'Whaaat!'

This time Brisker threw a glass ink bottle at Bytheway; then he threw a decanter, then a chair – all of which Bytheway fended off. Brisker was so angry that his motions were disjointed, as if he had splints down his trousers or the sleeves of his jacket.

It was clear that coming here had indeed been a mistake. Bytheway felt like a child who had climbed out upon a branch and could not get down. There could be no positive outcome, but he stayed because he was frightened to turn round. By degrees, however, Brisker slowed, and the wildness left his eyes. He was thinking. Bytheway stood and watched him, resisting an impulse to nurse his bruised cheek. His ink-stained suit, his bespattered shirt, infuriated him, but he did not show it and stood ready.

Presently Brisker stopped pacing, and smiled. 'You know, Mr Bytheway, someone told me that your bank was unsafe. You may know that I was on the point of investing in it, but someone warned me not to. I don't know the detail, but I wonder if you've been stealing funds as well as women.'

Bytheway had once stepped into the road before a cart and four big horses. As he had felt then, so he did now. 'Upon my honour. No, indeed. How dare you!'

Brisker continued to smile: how Bytheway wanted to slap him. Had he realised? 'I tell you, Mr Bytheway, that my wife will return to me, and I'll raise your child as my own. I'll find out, sooner or later, what you've done with her. She can have no life with you. A woman, Mr Bytheway, belongs to her husband, and she is mine. More than this, huh, huh, one way or another I'll ruin you. Perhaps I'll write to Mr Deacon and explain my apprehensions concerning his bank. At the least I'll mention your scandalous behaviour. Hardly the thing, is it, for a reputable establishment? May I suggest that your one hope is to return my wife to me? I'll give you a day or so to consider your options, but if you choose to delay you'll suffer for it. By whatever means, you'll be undone by my hand – either with the cosh or in some other manner. Goodnight, Mr Bytheway.'

He rang the bell and a stunned, bruised, ink-splattered Bytheway was shown to the door. He saw the maid glance at him. He pretended that he had come bruised and ink-splattered, and the servant was happy to pretend it, too. Just as Bytheway left the room his eyes met Brisker's. Perhaps involuntarily, Brisker raised his upper lip to show his teeth. He did something else, too, quite deliberately: he tickled the end of his nose with a quill, threatening to write to Deacon.

That night Bytheway went to Annie, and they began to plan for their escape. She was full of questions but he would not be distracted; matters were coming to a head. Could they flee before Brisker found Annie or wrote to Deacon? The sand was running low and fast in the hourglass, but they had a little time yet, he hoped.

Chapter Twenty-Eight

Bytheway was fiddling with some papers behind his desk. Woodhouse watched him, sure that the papers were private ones: his colleague always looked guilty when he was doing something private at work. This made Woodhouse curious, more so since he suspected Bytheway of consorting with Annie.

Bytheway was not good at doing anything untoward. He made some pretence of working, and Woodhouse enjoyed his discomfort. The hours that they spent together enabled them to read each other well, and each was much more transparent than he imagined. So it was that Woodhouse barely hid a smirk as Bytheway shuffled his papers and peered at them, and when Bytheway totted up a sum and signed a paper, how Woodhouse enjoyed that performance, too.

'Would you like me to add up those figures, Mr Bytheway?' asked Woodhouse sweetly. 'You seem to be struggling with them. Perhaps your mind is elsewhere today?' A cherub in a painting could not have been more innocent.

'No, no, I thank you, no,' said Bytheway, growing red about the cheeks. He shuffled the papers again, and Woodhouse looked at them. What was so interesting about those documents? Then, happily, something happened to distract Bytheway. Outside the bank's window a woman crossed the road just in front of a wagon pulled by two big horses. Although the driver brought the animals to a halt just in time, shouting as he did so, the old woman tripped on the pavement. She was slow to rise, and Bytheway went outside to help. Once she was upright again he became embroiled in a conversation. The papers lay unattended on his desk. Woodhouse looked at them, then at Bytheway just outside, and decided to read them. His heart thumped, as it always did when he behaved badly – but the risk of discovery was worthwhile.

Woodhouse could not believe his eyes. There were notes about passage overseas, a railway timetable, with Southampton marked, and a receipt for a hotel in Burton. A card with the papers confirmed that George had installed Annie there. The dog! Making a mistress of her! Carefully he put everything back as it had been and returned to his seat. He was calm and measured, but angry that Bytheway was planning to escape – apparently leaving him to carry the blame.

When Bytheway returned, Woodhouse was withdrawn but tried not to attract any attention. He was so diligent, in fact, that Bytheway did notice him, even asking him to stop for a moment so that he might be complimented upon his hard work.

'Thank you, Mr Bytheway,' said Woodhouse, although he despised Bytheway for his pettiness. Was Bytheway not about to abandon him and the bank? Had he not embezzled funds? And yet he still doled out compliments, like an old lady giving pennies to children. Sickening!

By and by Bytheway left the bank for the night. Before he went he stood and adjusted his tie. These days, more than ever, he was immaculate, and today he wore a spruce suit. His square-toed shoes gleamed, his trousers fitted him just so, and a watch chain gleamed in his waistcoat. He had a sort of dreamy quality too and a bloom about him. Mrs Brisker had certainly made a difference.

'Goodnight, Mr Bytheway,' said Woodhouse, glancing up.

'Goodnight, Horace. You need not work late. You may complete your work in the morning, if you wish.'

'Thank you, but I wish to have it done so that I may get on with other things.' For a moment his cheek quivered in his long, almond-shaped face, but he got up and bowed with great politeness before Bytheway bade him goodnight. The door shut behind him.

'Duffer,' said Woodhouse.

The silence in the bank was intense. Sunshine picked out the grain of the wood in the counter. The red tiles were warm in the early evening light. Ledgers in their rows showed brightly in their bindings. All was pleasing and well – but Woodhouse would turn this comfortable world upside down and shake it. Once Bytheway had left, Woodhouse speedily completed his work, which in truth he had all but done half an hour since. Then he took a fresh piece of paper. For a moment he thought, before beginning to write.

> Dear Mr Brisker,
>
> I write to you as a well wisher. The philanderer George Bytheway has secreted your wife in the Victoria Hotel at Burton. I believe, too, that Mr Bytheway is about to fly and intends to remove your wife overseas.
>
> A woman's place is in the home, sir, and our society may fall to pieces if home and hearth are to be undermined by seducers such as Mr Bytheway. If you were to catch him and cosh him as before who might blame you?
>
> I am a kind friend.

Woodhouse briefly resisted a flicker of guilt as he prepared his letter for the post. For a moment he considered destroying the note, but decided against it. He deplored Annie leaving 'home and hearth', which was odd, given the man he was. It was bizarre that apart from anger and jealousy he was motivated by indignation. He would have been shocked had he realised what a prig he could be.

By way of justification, Woodhouse brooded upon Bytheway as a seducer and a home-wrecker, but there was also some prurience in his thoughts. He was strongly drawn toward Annie, and the memory of her naked that day in his rooms stirred him. He pictured her on her back, and contemplated her in her passion with George. It insulted him that she might prefer Bytheway. This last thought, together with Bytheway's intention to escape and his decision not to steal again convinced Woodhouse to post the letter. Like a shower of rain in April, his guilt about sending the letter was swift in passing. As he committed it to the post a little thrill ran through him as he contemplated what might come of it.

Chapter Twenty-Nine

Annie had all but her necessaries packed and was almost ready to leave. She was desperate to go; while she remained in the hotel she had a sense of being overtaken by events. The day was fine and pleasant, and people were courteous, but a sense of something amiss tracked her like a dog.

Once Bytheway left that morning she went out herself: she had some errands and wished to be busy. Later she found a pleasant spot and sat to ponder, before deciding to return to her rooms. Unknown to her, the train from Lichfield was approaching. With every belch of smoke it brought Brisker nearer. He, too, was heading for her rooms.

Annie would not be happy until she saw Bytheway again, and, more particularly, until they escaped. That night she would plead with him to go immediately: never mind if he were not ready, they must run. It was such an adventure: who would have thought that her life would have taken this course? She was to be a mother too. She loved Bytheway and loved the child she carried. If only they might get away so the three of them could grow to the sun together.

On the way back to the hotel Annie chanced to meet a friend, and the two women took tea together as the train arrived from Lichfield. Like a devil in sulphur fumes, Brisker emerged from the smoke and steam of the train and made his way directly to the Victoria Hotel.

A little later Annie returned to her accommodation, but on the way back she lingered, finding distraction in the least thing. The foreboding that she had had all day was strong in her now, so strong that she hesitated at her door, standing for a moment with the key in her hand. At length, however, she put it in the lock, turned it and entered. Everything was as it had been, but there was the sense of something. Just then someone cleared his throat, softly, behind her. Annie knew who it was. She turned round, planning her next move, knowing that he was between her and the door; and there he was.

Brisker looked at her and she at him. Holding his straight-sided top hat, wearing an open coat and waistcoat, cravat and braces, fashionable checked wool trousers and shiny shoes, with his hair short and side-parted, he was entirely respectable; quite the gentleman.

'You left me, Anne.' He looked like a child admonishing a parent who was late coming to collect him from school.

'Have you come to kill me?' She found his strange, stone eyes. 'Don't kill me, Mr Brisker. I'm having a child.'

'Ha,' he snapped. This had not been tactful. She was worried, though, not for her life but for her child's. 'Ha!'

Annie flinched. Some of the colour drained from her, her black brows and her hair seeming darker against her white face. Much good was her green travelling dress now, her packed bags. 'I'll scream if you try to harm me.'

'How fecund,' said Brisker, ignoring the question of violence. 'Is he more of a man than me, huh, huh? Is that why you left me, to procreate with him?'

'I left you because you routinely betrayed me with prostitutes, Mr Brisker,' she said, calmly. 'Because you force-fed me, subjected me to the water treatment, treated me as a brood mare, bullied, terrorised and finally beat me. That is why I left you.'

'No, no. You are a harlot. You and Bytheway. Did he tumble you, huh, huh? Please you? Did he please you as I could not? On our bed, perhaps? Huh, huh? Did you entertain him there? Did you? Did you?'

'I did not,' she said. 'There was nothing improper between Mr Bytheway and me – if you call it that – until after you raised your hand to me and I left your house.'

Brisker muttered through his teeth. He raised his hand and Annie hunched, expecting a blow; but he let his hand fall again.

'Our marriage', she said, breathing deeply, 'is over. I desire that you release me so that I may marry Mr Bytheway.'

'No,' said Brisker, shaking his head. 'No.' He seemed to bunch his face up; his eyes became small, lines creased at their corners and his mouth almost appeared to turn inside out. This was something that she had never seen in him before. Once she might have been moved to see him trying not to cry. Now she stood and watched, expecting violence when he collected himself. Her husband raised his hands to his face, and breathed heavily through them. For a moment Annie thought that he was going to leave, quietly, without fuss.

'Annie,' he said, 'I love you.'

'Desist.'

'I love you,' he said, raising his eyes to hers. 'Heaven knows that I'm a bad man, Annie, I know that, but I love you. You cannot leave me. You cannot begin again with another man.'

'I've done so, Mr Brisker.'

'My name is John, Anne. John – and I'm your husband!'

'I've begun again,' she said. 'I'm carrying another man's child, and I'm happy.'

'I could make you happy!' he cried. 'I'll raise your child as my own. A man wants an heir, huh, huh?'

'No.'

'You have no choice, Anne. I'll not release you, and the law doesn't allow you to divorce me. Your property, money, all that

169

you brought to our marriage, belongs to me. You belong to me. Your man, Bytheway, will soon be in jail. I know now that he is an embezzler. When you warned me to remove my money from Deacon's bank the warning came from him. You told me that it was one of your gutter friends, one of your drinking club, but it was him. How stupid I was not to realise it sooner. Bytheway would be in jail by now had I done so, but he shall be in jail directly. Tomorrow I intend to expose him. How shall you support yourself with your man in jail? You would have no money and you would fall into degradation. Your child would be taken from you. You would find yourself in the workhouse and your child would become a pauper. On the other hand, I intend to bring up your child as my own. He shall be given my name and will never know that I'm not his natural father. You must never tell him otherwise. You have no choice, Anne.'

The truth of this seemed to be unanswerable. Annie sank back onto the bed. She sat on the covers, turned over what he had said and, while he watched her, cried, hands raised to her face. Brisker was not unsympathetic: he let her cry, and even looked a little moved as great sobs shook her. He even went so far as to pass her a handkerchief.

Poor Annie. She had escaped, and now the cell door slammed shut upon her again. Her new life disappeared; the old one replaced it. She would not raise her child with its father, the man she loved. There would be no escape. She must betray Bytheway, and be gone when he next came to see her. She cried again.

'Come,' he said.

'Please,' she begged, brows knitted, 'I will come with you now, but don't expose Mr Bytheway.'

Brisker was non-committal. 'Perhaps.'

'I beg you not to expose him.'

'Perhaps.'

'I must write a note for Mr Bytheway.'

'One minute.'

Frantically she cast round for paper, ink and pen. Brisker was looking at his pocket watch, so she only wrote a few words.

My Dear George,
Mr Brisker has come for me and I have no
choice but to return to him.

'Come,' he said again. She scribbled a few more words. 'Come!'
Just as she was about to tell Bytheway that she loved him Brisker
made it clear that his patience had ended. She wrote her name,
then he took the pen from her. She folded the note, ready to leave
it downstairs – where Brisker had already settled her account.
There was a moment while Annie collected herself, dried her
eyes, composed herself – respectability was the watchword – and
so, at last, tolerably correctly, they left together, decorously, like
the man and wife they were. Only once did Annie, gaunt and
looking older than her years, look behind her.

Chapter Thirty

Bytheway was on his way to the hotel just as Annie left it. The nearer he approached, the further from it she was, and all his hustle and bustle counted for nothing. Their room in the hotel was empty and no trace of them remained in it, but in his mind she was there and waiting for him. In fact, his train passed Annie's along the way and, as his father might have said, Bytheway would arrive just in time to be too late. Thus the tickets in his wallet and the plans in his head were useless. There was a purse in his pocket which was also superfluous now, and a case to be unpacked, and a thousand and one disappointments waiting for him; but of course he did not know yet that Annie had gone. So it was that he was full of plans for escape, and his exhilaration blew like the wind in his sails all the way to Burton.

Of course, he was mortified about the bank. He could not bear to think what people would say of him, but he had explained himself to Deacon in a letter which he would post before they left. He had not dwelt in his letter upon Deacon's provocation, and expressed the hope that Deacon might ride out any scandal and carry on. Bytheway suggested, too, that the embezzlement had been his alone, something which Woodhouse scarcely deserved.

The motion of the train invigorated Bytheway. He loved to be going somewhere, and enjoyed seeing the countryside pass the window. By the time the train reached Burton he was feeling optimistic, and went directly to the Victoria Hotel. He hurried along, and the closer he got the more his mood rose. The nearness of Annie thrilled him. By the time the hotel was in view he was almost running, and he quite bounded up the steps into the familiar lobby.

Bytheway was surprised when a call from the desk interrupted him – irritated, too. He wanted to see Annie. A little impatiently he returned to the desk.

The person who had called him over had a sort of syrup of figs or cod liver oil manner, as if he had just that moment swallowed a whole tablespoonful of the stuff and struggled to stomach it. 'Mrs Brisker left this note for you, sir. Had we known about your arrangement, may I say that neither you nor Mrs Brisker would have been welcome here.' As if the man's underwear were too tight he minced to a cabinet behind his desk and produced a note with a flourish. He thrust it at Bytheway, and resumed his business. Clearly Mr George Bytheway was no longer welcome.

Despite the hostility, Bytheway took the note to a wooden bench that sat in the light of the big bay windows. His hand shook as he took it, and at first he could not bring himself to read it. What was the point? He knew what it said. He felt his stomach turn. How it would have pleased Bytheway if he had spewed then, spewed all over the lobby. His moral guardian behind the desk would really have had something to complain about. The man continued to squint at him, and so Bytheway read the note.

> My Dear George,
> Mr Brisker has come for me and I have no
> choice but to return to him. I have no
> choice.
> One last thing. He has guessed about

the bank but may, I hope, spare you public exposure.

Annie

So brief! She did not even say that she loved him. She did not even say that she loved him! He could hardly bear it. As if he might understand it differently he continued to stare, stupidly, at the note.

'I must ask you, sir, to vacate our lobby.' The clerk drew himself up, swaying his head from side to side and pursing his lips, not unlike a snake drawn from its coil by a charmer.

'Be quiet, sir,' shouted Bytheway, 'unless you want to feel my fists. Do you? You know nothing about it, sir. Nothing!'

The man pulled a face, and wriggled away, his head wobbling as if it were loose.

It was time for Bytheway to leave. He got up and wandered out into the street. There were people in the street. He was oddly aware that some of the passers-by looked at him. He did not know why he attracted them. He hardly knew what he did but, somehow, found his way back to the station. He might easily have caught a train to anywhere; in fact, he had no memory of boarding a train at all but, incredibly, got home. He briefly considered going to a pub but decided against it, and wandered a little, but people bothered him. He went home and tried to pray, but finally went to bed, put out his light – and the blackness swallowed him whole.

Chapter Thirty-One

The next morning at the bank Bytheway was there in person only; his attention was elsewhere and his mind wandered at the smallest opportunity, so that Woodhouse, wearing a lop-sided grin, watched him and laughed.

In Bytheway's mind he was in bed with Annie, the night before their final parting. That night they had lain long and discussed their escape. They had already plotted their route and knew, too, their ship, which would now sail without them. To think of it: just a few days would have done it. They would have escaped.

How Annie had held him tightly that last morning. He had made light of this affection, he remembered, but had wrapped one arm around her and stroked her head with his other hand. Bytheway stroked his hand now as he thought of it, recalling, too, how she had looked at him. She had seemed to map every inch, as if knowing that they would never see each other again.

'You're very handsome, Mr Bytheway,' he said, repeating Annie's words to him. 'You're very handsome, Mr Bytheway.'

He was no longer remembering; he was re-living. He smiled and felt again overwhelmed, as always, with the sense of Annie.

She seemed so real that he could feel her touch. He might have cried to remember how they had parted but, jaunty, trying for levity, he had broken free, turned and gone, expecting to see her later, which was something which would be denied him ever again.

'Are you well, George?' said Deacon suddenly. 'George!'

Deacon suddenly materialised from nowhere and began shaking Bytheway. Woodhouse laughed. This time, Deacon or no Deacon, Woodhouse laughed. Deacon shot a fierce glance at him.

'Any further levity from you, sir, and you will leave my employ in the same minute. Come along.' He returned to Bytheway and gave him a slap. 'You were telling yourself that you were handsome,' he said.

'The apothecary made up a mixture for me, sir. I'm afraid that it may be too strong for me. Forgive me, I am quite myself now,' lied Bytheway. Had he usually been puce-coloured he might have looked himself again, but he was ordinarily pale pink. Deacon peered at him like a cat seen from a mousehole, while behind him Woodhouse seemed ready to burst. Only providence saved Bytheway; the door bell jangled.

'A customer, sir.'

Respectability was everything in their society. In the bank respectability was doubly important. Before the customer, Deacon made light of the fact that he had been shaking his clerk. He chortled, and even gave Bytheway a pat on the cheek. Oh, what a lark! With a last chuckle he trotted off to his office.

And so it was that the day went on. People came to the counter; people went. Bytheway did things through habit, without knowing that he did them, and said things too in a similar fashion. Extraordinarily he did his bookwork without error or conscious thought. The morning trudged into the afternoon. Deacon left. He had business elsewhere and went for the day. Meanwhile, Woodhouse waited his chance. Waiting tormented him, but finally the ins and outs of customers lessened and ceased, at least for a moment. They took to their ledgers, and then Woodhouse could contain himself no longer.

'Do you know that you were talking to yourself? You repeated

"You're very handsome, Mr Bytheway" twice! You had no idea when Deacon entered. I rose to bow to him and you were talking to yourself. I'm sorry, old man, but I had to laugh. What's the matter, George?'

Bytheway looked at him narrowly. 'Brisker has stolen Annie from me. He found out where she was and recovered her.'

'Oooh.'

'Oooh,' parroted Bytheway. This was a pivotal moment. 'I've something else to tell you, too.'

'What do you mean?'

'Annie left me a note yesterday. Brisker knows. He knows everything.'

'Tell me!'

'I warned Annie about the bank. I wanted to protect her, lest Brisker lose his funds if the bank collapsed. She told him that one of her drinking friends had mentioned it, but he realised who had told her.'

'You damned fool!'

Like a plughole, Woodhouse's open mouth consumed the last of his good humour. He covered his eyes with his hands.

'But Annie has asked him not to expose us.'

'Oh, thank God.'

One, two, three. Bytheway waited his moment. 'But I don't trust him.' He removed Woodhouse's hope, like a sheet in a conjuring trick. He enjoyed the unkindness. 'You see,' he said, 'he'll spare us nothing. What a shame. What a dreadful, dreadful shame. Do you not think that it's a dreadful shame, Horace?' He found Woodhouse's dodging eyes. 'If only Brisker had not discovered Annie. Was it not unfortunate, Horace, that Mr Brisker discovered her?'

This sarcasm hung in the air. The seconds ticked by until Woodhouse accepted it, like an kiss from a wrinkly aunt.

'Oh!'

He took to his feet and began pacing. 'So you mean to punish me. So that's why you didn't warn me. How could you? I would be onboard ship to Canada by now.'

Ordinarily Woodhouse seldom surprised Bytheway, but he did so now. As Woodhouse felt betrayed, his own letter to Brisker seemed a trifle. His eyes, in staring at Bytheway, were like knots in a piece of wood. 'Judas! Shall I call you that, George? Judas!'

'You! You talk to me of treachery!'

'Were you not about to leave? I saw your preparations in those papers upon your desk.'

'No!' said Bytheway. 'Fool as I am I would have warned you first.'

' Mr Bytheway,' said Woodhouse. 'Liar!'

Bytheway turned his back, although Woodhouse was oblivious of Bytheway. He put his hands over his eyes and through his hair. He stopped pacing and sat down but got up. He sat down again, then resumed pacing: back and forth, back and forth.

'Must think. Must think. Too clever. Too clever.' Woodhouse's solution when it occurred to him was predictable enough. 'Of course!' He pointed to Bytheway. 'Tell them that it was your doing. Tell them that I knew nothing about it.'

'What?'

The seconds ticked by.

'No.'

'I'm not meant to have any access to the notes. They would believe that it was your doing.'

'No.'

'Tell them!'

'No.'

Woodhouse could not believe Bytheway's selfishness. 'I cannot go to prison.'

Their conversation, which had been fraught, now took a turn towards farce. Picture a harvest festival turnip, with a chiselled mouth and bodged eyes: so it was with Woodhouse. Suddenly there was a touch upon Bytheway's knee.

'No!' Bytheway jumped to his feet. He was shouting now, no longer the gentleman. 'You've brought this upon us. You!' For a moment he had his own hands up through his hair. 'You, when you told Brisker where to find Anne.'

Woodhouse absorbed this information. He seemed to want to deny his guilt. A little pantomime of conflicting thoughts passed behind his eyes. Suddenly, there was another touch upon Bytheway's knee.

'No!' Bytheway wrenched him to his feet. 'Come, we'll share the blame between us.'

Tick-tock, tick-tock, tick-tock. The clock took this opportunity to say something. Tick-tock, tick-tock.

The idea of responsibility appalled Woodhouse. 'No!' He gained the most wondrous eyes, wide, white. He looked at Bytheway like one of the apostles in a Bible story. 'How can I sit here and wait to be arrested? I know you. You mean to escape and leave me to carry the blame.'

'I don't.'

'You mean to cheat me,' said Woodhouse.

'No.'

'I shall go to Deacon now and tell him. Tell him that you're a cheat and an embezzler.'

'No.'

'I shall! I shall say that I've entertained suspicions about you for some while and now am sure.'

'No!'

Bytheway jumped up and took Woodhouse by the shoulders. 'No, control yourself man.' He began to shake him, when the door opened. Somehow Bytheway was invested in that moment with a sort of unnatural power. He knew who had entered; somehow Woodhouse knew who it was, too. None the less, the second or so while the door swung open was an agony to them both. Who else might it have been than a certain small, black haired gentleman?

'Oh, I'm sorry to interrupt you, gentlemen,' he said, smiling. 'I can see, huh, that you're having a private moment.'

They saw him as they would a jailer, as if he had been jangling keys. In that moment he seemed like judge and jury too. There was a moment of stasis. The three men looked at one another. Woodhouse was first to act. Rubbing his hands together, he slunk over to their visitor. He showed his teeth, too; his eyes were huge. He resisted the temptation to touch Brisker, but his hand rubbing gathered pace. Bytheway watched. Brisker watched. 'It was I who told you where to find your wife. Will you tell them that it was all his fault?'

The words sank in. Like an engine, which nods to pump water from a mine, Brisker rocked and absorbed this request. Woodhouse and Bytheway, too, watched him. Suddenly a smile, like a benediction, spread slowly over Brisker's face. 'I'm obliged to you,' he said.

Woodhouse was so limp with relief that he flopped down. He was so happy that he shed a tear or two. He was unembarrassed by this display, too: oh, to escape! After a moment or two, however, he sat up. He was now quite another person and seemed keen to watch what happened next.

'Woodhouse!' said Bytheway. 'How could you? How could you do this to me?'

'The rats are deserting the ship, are they not?' said Brisker.

Bytheway found it hard even to look at Brisker, but turned two weary eyes on him. 'At last,' he said, 'we find something to agree upon.'

Tick-tock, tick-tock, tick-tock. One of those long moments dragged out when nothing was said or done, until Brisker approached the door. The hope that he might leave them was soon disappointed, however. Brisker did not leave but turned the key. Turning back, he savoured their discomfort, turned it round in his mouth and sucked it. He appeared to read them, and to be attuned to their thoughts. In truth, however, perhaps they read him, too, and so they deduced that he seemed to wait for something. Bytheway was desperate and Brisker almost orchestrated what happened next.

'You needn't inform upon us, Mr Brisker ...'

'Yes,' nodded Brisker, 'Yes.'

'Annie's already returned to your house ...'

'Yes, and what of it?'

'Please, be so good as to leave us now.'

The plea was made. The drumming of Brisker's fingers upon his cheek denoted his consideration of this request. Bytheway and Woodhouse watched him carefully. Brisker put a hand to his mouth and pondered, but he only pretended to deliberate. 'Ha!' he shouted. 'Is that the best you can do? I told Annie that I'd have you beg and I have. Ha!'

'Then damn you, sir!' said Bytheway, 'I retract it. Do your worst.'

'Oh,' said Brisker, 'I shall! I mean to destroy you. And you, rat.' Woodhouse sat up. 'I'll destroy you into the bargain.'

Had Bytheway been minded to laugh he might have done so now. Brisker did laugh. Woodhouse put his hands on his hips. He even stamped and turned to Bytheway. 'I told him where to find his wife!'

It was left to Brisker to explain. 'You cannot think that I respect you,' he said.

Like a stone dropped into a well, this remark did not register at once, but it made a splash at last and then they fell into silence, which marked the end of their business. The clerks stood on the brink of public exposure. For a moment more they were respectable: chief clerk and junior clerk together and then Brisker unlocked the door and stepped outside. In Bore Street people came and went: smart couples on smart horses, delivery vehicles, gentlemen raising hats to ladies, shoppers going window to window, gossipers, a child with a hoop and stick, and more. Brisker stepped off the pavement, and came to rest in the middle of the street. The traffic had to stop for him. People began to stare. Someone shouted. Then Brisker opened his mouth. 'Mr Deacon's bank is unsafe! George Bytheway is a thief! Bytheway has been stealing Mr Deacon's funds. Mr Bytheway is an embezzler. Mr Bytheway is a thief. Deacon's bank is unsafe.'

'If you're going to try and get away, Horace,' said Bytheway kindly, 'you must go now.' Woodhouse raised his head and saw that Bytheway was right. Outside a crowd was gathering. The traffic had stopped and, on left and right, was beginning to coalesce. People had joined Brisker in the road. White-eyed, Woodhouse took to his heels. He hoped to flee by train, or run, and so he clattered across the floor to the doorway and fled down the street. It may be said that this occurrence ruffled the bystanders. There was a 'hue and cry', as it would once have been called. A clerk taking to his heels did not much soothe the crowd, as one might know.

'Run,' thought Bytheway. As he watched, a few people left the crowd and gave chase. 'Run,' called out Bytheway.

When he could no longer see Woodhouse, Bytheway turned and looked once to Woodhouse's chair and empty desk. The irony of it, that he should miss him. Another irony occurred to Bytheway too, that he could be lonely: outside were many people whom he knew. He had an impulse to tell the crowd how this farce had occurred, but instead locked the door. Within seconds of the key being turned someone tried the handle. More people came forward to try the door. Then there came a bump-bump-bump summons upon it.

'Open this door, Mr Bytheway!'

A kind of note went up among the crowd; Bytheway could hear it from within. It was a sort of whine, not a human noise at all but animal and primal. All those with money in the bank contemplated losing it: sharp-elbowed officers of the Militia on half pay; members of the Corporation, fretting for the proceeds of their threepenny rate; clerics and shopkeepers; gentlemen investors; merchants; pensioners; ladies in lop-sided bonnets; farmers and professional men; artisans; undertakers; Mr Jukes, the apothecary; Mr Lee, the priest; even Bytheway's housekeeper, poor old thing; all pushed and jostled and shouted, and still they banged on the door. Across the road there were children watching, some of the children from the workhouse with their matron. Just a short while ago they had sung his praises.

'Open this door, Mr Bytheway. Explain yourself. This cannot be true. Open the door!'

Bytheway pondered how he had come to find himself there against the bank door. Was he really there, besieged inside the bank? Surely all this was a dream from which he would wake with a start. But the thumps upon the wood were real enough. He imagined the horror of all those people who summoned him. They must struggle to believe what they had heard, and Bytheway grieved for his good name. Pray God that the workhouse children were not made cynical through his shortcomings.

As the banging on the door continued, Bytheway sat with his back to the panels but finally moved to the window. As he looked out, Deacon appeared, pushing, shoving, making his red-faced way through the crowd, his hat almost knocked sideways.

'George!' came the familiar voice. 'Open this door at once. What's the matter with you, man? Open it!'

Bytheway recognised the panic in the familiar voice. Deacon was desperate, and wanted him to say that this riot was not what it appeared to be. By little verbal clues he led Bytheway, trying to extrude reassurance. 'George, please! George?' He yearned for Bytheway to make it untrue, but Bytheway could not do that because it was true.

'I'm sorry, Mr Deacon, I beg you to forgive me. I've betrayed you.'

Silence.

'I've betrayed you'.

Silence.

'I've betrayed you.'

'What!' This was too much to believe. Nor did Deacon wish anyone else, standing near, to believe it.

'I betrayed you,' shouted Bytheway.

'No, not you!'

'You tried to rob me of my faith,' shouted Bytheway. 'I was so angry.'

'George.'

'I was going to kill myself, Mr Deacon. Do you hear that? I was going to kill myself, but then I thought that I'd hurt you, as you see now. You've had a hand in it. I started to steal the cancelled notes and spend them. To this date I have taken £7,350.'

Seven thousand, three hundred and fifty pounds! Seven thousand, three hundred and fifty pounds! Deacon wanted to be sick, he wanted to kill Bytheway and he wanted to run. The three thoughts jostled in his mind, but he also thought of his assets. His total assets exceeded that amount. If only he could prevent a run on the bank. In that moment Deacon summoned himself. He had to ride out the crisis. 'Good people,' he said. He turned and faced the crowd. 'Good people.' He showed his teeth like a monkey, the apples shining in his cheeks. 'Good people.' The crowd at last became silent, and Deacon lifted his hands. 'Mr Bytheway is unwell. Such is his attention to duty that he's quite overset to have mislaid some trifling amount. Be not alarmed. No one will lose a farthing, not one farthing, but I beg you, in your Christian charity, not to remove your money from my bank. We must avoid a run upon the bank! My resources are such that I can easily make good the shortfall. However, if everyone comes at once for their money I'll be ruined. You'd find the bank closed, all accounts suspended and subject to bankruptcy proceedings. Be rational! We're not animals; we do not need to climb over one another to take our bite from a carcase! No, be patient and all may be well. Let there be no run on my bank. Go home and be not alarmed.'

The people outside the bank, crammed into the space around the bank's door, glanced at one another. Each one tried to guess the intentions of the others; each one tried to hide their own feelings, but among them all one thought was uppermost: if there was going to be a run on the bank each meant to be first to withdraw their money. Deacon tried to read their intentions, too. None the less, he stretched out his arms and smiled, hanging a grin like a hammock from his shiny cheekbones. He was softly spoken too, matter of fact. The matter was of no great import. A blow to the head, such as Bytheway had suffered recently, might produce such distemper.

'Go home, please. Go home.' He shook his head; he gestured. He implied, 'What was there to do?' 'Carry on your business,' he said. 'There's nothing to see here and no cause for worry.'

By the time the last of the people around him had dispersed Deacon's arms were weary, but at last he had managed to placate them. Unwillingly they left, in dribs and drabs, until only Deacon and Bytheway remained, with a door between them. So it was that, for the moment, the ordinary commerce of the street and the city resumed. The activities of Lichfield continued as before, the comings and the goings, all the ordinary way of things, except that Deacon could not get into his bank. Poor Deacon. For as long as he maintained his calm exterior his heart had been pounding. His round, bewhiskered face, with its red cheeks, belied the sense of dread which was building in him, and finally he went too. Poor Deacon.

'Be a good chap, George, there's a good fellow,' he said through the door, just before he left. 'We don't want to cause a fuss; it might damage the bank and we don't want that, do we? Come out, lock the door behind you, make your way to the Guildhall and surrender to a constable.'

Behind the door Bytheway heard this and could not believe it. He wanted to go on being George Bytheway, senior clerk, earning £400 a year and respected wherever he went. He did not want to go from here, from all he knew and go to jail.

He prepared to leave the bank and gathered himself. He straightened the papers on his desk, as if he would be coming back. Finally he put his hands together and got down on one knee. Through disbelief and theft and adultery somehow he had found grace. Even now he felt the presence of the Lord: the straight way lay before him. He must surrender and make reparation for his embezzlement and so, sadly, he opened the door, carefully locked it again and, like a picture of respectability, went to the Guildhall and surrendered to a constable.

Chapter Thirty-Two

I t was after one in the morning and Lichfield was quiet, although somewhere a dog barked. There were lights in odd windows but Lichfield slept. Certainly along Dam Street the houses slept, their blinds like the lids of poultry sleeping all along a perch. Meanwhile, like a fox in the night, Deacon wandered the streets, aimless, but when he got to Minster Pool he stopped.

There was a bright, cold moon riding the skies, drifting between silvered clouds and a shadow stretched behind Deacon on the bank. The moon reached down and drew its hand across the water but otherwise the pool looked black and deep.

By day Minster Pool was a lovely spot. There were fine trees along the bank, which ran across the Close gardens. These trees, and the houses beyond them, were black outlines now. Even the cathedral was reduced to a silhouette, and the whole Close lay denuded of colour and life. At such an hour the Close seemed to be detached from the present. It was easy to think of the years gone by and all the many dramas which had occurred there, such as in the Civil War. Many, many people had died hereabouts during the sieges of the Cathedral. Such thoughts brought to mind the ghost which Bytheway had reported. Even Deacon felt this sense of the past. The Close was unfit now for a man of flesh and blood, alone while all the world slept except for him.

When all this was said, however, Deacon wished to be alone and, as he stood by the pool, he had a purpose. Deacon wore one of his expensive suits and over that an expensive coat. The pockets of suit and coat were full of stones, so many that the pockets bulged. His trousers, too, contained stones, and his waistcoat was padded with stones, and he carried stones in his hands.

That day the following advertisement had appeared in the Lichfield press:

> Stowe House, Lichfield
> The premises and property of J.W. Deacon (bankrupt) is to be sold by auction at the George Hotel, Lichfield, on September 23rd, 1860, at 1.30 in the afternoon, by order of the assignees of Mr John W. Deacon, bankrupt, in several lots.
>
> The mansion house, called Stowe House, is most pleasingly situated near to Stowe Church and provides fine views across Stowe Pool towards Lichfield Cathedral. The house is surrounded by a well-kept lawn, planted with shrubs and flowers, with glasshouses and a kitchen garden. In total, including land adjoining, the house possesses grounds of 10a 3r. 38p. freehold, with further land rented on leases from the Cathedral Church of Lichfield on most generous terms.
>
> The house comprises drawing and dining rooms, a study, library, five large bedrooms and seven smaller rooms, three

water closets, servants' accommodation –
sufficient for a staff of ten – bakehouse,
brewhouse, laundry, dairy, farm
buildings, stabling, outbuildings,
coachhouses, plus a goldfish pool and fowl
pens.

The advertisement went on to list the contents of the house,
which were also to be sold: furniture, musical instruments, silver
and plated goods, a camera, china, linen, several fine watches,
rare, curious and expensive books, cut glass, clothes, hats and
footwear, wine, paintings, carriages, prints, and so on. The
advertisement allocated a day for different types of goods, until
the sale culminated on the twelfth day with removables from the
servants' quarters. In short, very nearly all Deacon had, all his
possessions, were hawked in a public auction – leaving him with
all but nothing. The law allowed him little more than the clothes
which he wore on his back.

The water was cold as Deacon stepped into it. He shuddered,
even shrank from the chill, but kept on. On the bottom were
stones, and he began to make deliberate passage out to the
deeper water. He trod carefully, which was odd – because he
intended to kill himself. The water began to seep up his clothing.
The weight of his coat tails was shocking, and his trousers
wrapped around him like reeds. Almost against his will, he began
to breathe in short, truncated gasps as the water passed through
his coat and suit, and his shirt and the vest under that, and played
against his skin. The stones in his pockets threatened to overset
him. Once he fell there would be no regaining his footing, even if
the flesh were weak and he tried to save himself.

Perhaps his senses were quickened, but of a sudden Deacon
noticed something. In that moment the moonlight caught his
eyes. He followed something on the bank, away towards Dam
Street. Whatever it was across the water seemed to take note of
him. Years of scepticism flashed across his mind, but it seemed
that the horseman had come for him. In the water, in the

191

moonlight, like one of the trees on the margin of the pool, he stood transfixed. His next conscious thought was of movement on the bank behind him. There was a noise, then someone seized his arm. Deacon screamed. He lashed out in the water, which thrashed about him. He almost slipped but, rudely, roughly, as if life were something worth having, Deacon found himself dragged to the bank.

'Stop this, Mr Deacon. What were you thinking of? Come out, sir.' It was one of the city policemen. 'Come on, sir; come on.'

Like children tied together in a party game they staggered out, sloshing, but the bank was mossy. Repeatedly they fell back in, until, finally, Deacon escaped and hauled PC Wagstaff up after him. They were out: out! One looked at the other. Neither one knew what to say. In lieu of conversation, one helped the other: brushing detritus away, for example; but eventually Wagstaff looked at Deacon. Deacon looked at the hand on his shoulder and then slowly raised his own hands to his face. This expedient of raising his hands seemed childish, a petty evasion, and Wagstaff thought of pulling Deacon's hands away, but Deacon was sobbing. In fact, Deacon vented a great deal of emotion, which arose from various things, not just his bankruptcy. Strangely he had no sense of embarrassment. Indeed, he was then so lonely that he only heard Wagstaff as if the policeman were far removed.

There was an interval, during which Wagstaff minded his own business, and time, but it was Deacon who spoke first.

'Did you see it?' Deacon pointed.

'What, sir?'

'The horseman.' Deacon looked like a prophet from the desert, wide-eyed, dirty and heedless of earthly things. He was bedraggled, tousled, covered in mud, slimed in moss and his clothing torn, but the wonder never left him.

Wagstaff tut-tutted and shook his head. 'I saw nothing, sir. Perhaps you saw me. Now listen.' He bent down. His moustache and mutton chop whiskers made him look fierce, especially as he grimaced as he resisted the cold, but his eyes were kind. Once again a companionable hand settled on Deacon's shoulder. 'I

192

know that things haven't gone well for you, sir, but there's no call for this. You must get back to work. A man of your energy and intelligence will soon enough be on his feet again, maybe not as before, but respectable, sir, and independent. I know as you've lost near all you had, but money isn't everything.'

'Not everything!' Deacon embraced this thought as if it were the Wisdom of the Ancients. It seemed a sort of revelation to him, and once more, again open-mouthed, he stared towards where he thought he had seen the ghost.

'There's no one over there, sir,' said Wagstaff. 'Nothing and nobody. Now, you get back to your lodgings, sir.'

So he was sent to his bed like a child. Deacon briefly considered the altered way of things and shook his head; however, he would not kill himself, but would try to build his life as before, despite the years he carried on his back, his latent illness, lack of funds and so on, but he would try. Deacon straightened his attire once more, as if to make himself respectable. Indeed, as if he wanted approval, Deacon suddenly looked to the policeman and Wagstaff nodded. Each looked at the other for a moment, and then they shook hands.

'After all,' said Deacon, 'a man such as J.W. Deacon must always rise uppermost.'

'Yes, sir,' said Wagstaff.

After a civil goodnight, Deacon walked off, muddy, trailing water behind him, but trying to keep his head up and to walk like a gentleman.

Chapter Thirty-Three

When Bytheway came before the Quarter Sessions Court he pleaded guilty, and the trial was not drawn-out. In mitigation he mentioned Deacon's provocation and explained to the court that he had been driven to punish him. Many people sympathised, as Bytheway described how Deacon had scourged him. Bytheway explained how science had weakened his belief, and that Deacon's attacks were like a lash to a bare back. Deacon listened and said nothing; nor did anything about him disclose his thoughts. Likewise, he was emotionless when Bytheway stood for sentence: four years' penal servitude. Four years.

Bytheway said a few words before he was taken below. He apologised to Deacon, who remained expressionless, and to the bank's customers. He begged people to forgive him, if they could, and added that he had found his faith again. He deserved his punishment, he said, but hoped that his faith would uphold him, both in prison and in the harsh world that awaited him once he was released.

So it was that George Bytheway, former chief clerk, was taken down to begin his sentence. In leaving the court, he wanted to behave as a gentleman, and did exactly that. To the last he kept his back straight and head up. Finally he looked around him, perhaps hoping that Annie was there. She was not, but Brisker watched him. Bytheway disappeared from view. Justice had been served.

As Bytheway's head slipped from view, it may have seemed that the matter was over, but for him it had just begun. Even while he could still hear footfalls in the court, he was received into the keeping of the Prison Service. Minutes after his sentence he stepped into a secure van, alighting from it inside prison. Once there he stripped naked and submitted to an examination; likewise he gave up his clothes, and, without being asked, handed over his possessions. A stone-faced warden gave him a parcel of clothes and Bytheway put them on, ignoring the irritation to his skin. Likewise, he tried to accept being spoken to brusquely. He did not complain, but he was wretched, and the time dragged, from the first minute when the cell door shut upon him. However, there were sixty minutes in each hour and twenty-four hours in a day and seven days in a week, and so on, and so he began to count. This was how he survived: getting through the next minute and the one after that. Whatever they did to him they could not make more than sixty minutes in the hour. His sentence could be measured in minutes or in hours, and he set about ticking them off, one after another.

So much for Bytheway. But, of course, he was not the only person affected. The collapse of the bank hurt many people, and was not easily forgotten or made good. Deacon, newly bankrupt, decided to leave Lichfield – because, ironically, a Christian (unknown to him) had offered him a place in a bank. Deacon was to be a senior clerk. He would have left earlier, but had delayed to see his former clerks convicted. However, the court accepted Woodhouse's defence that he was innocent of embezzlement: he successfully argued that he had run away from the bank on the day it collapsed only because he feared for his life, because he thought there would be a riot. At Woodhouse's acquittal Deacon reacted like an old ginger tabby cat irritated by a flea, shaking his head violently. He knew that Woodhouse was guilty; indeed, he would not have been surprised to find out that Woodhouse had originated the plan.

Thus it was that Woodhouse, barely able to contain himself, left the court a free man, his sly grin and slanting, ebullient eyes restrained only until he was outside the building. He celebrated that night with alcohol and a prostitute, and soon afterward emigrated. At last he began his new life, setting sail for America – disappointed in his request that Deacon should give him a reference.

Little did Woodhouse know that the Civil War was brewing. Had he been better informed he might have avoided the American South, drawn, as he was, by stories of the river boats. But then, he might have thought that he was too clever, too slippery, too spry to be caught up in it. He was not too clever, too slippery or too spry to escape the conflict as things turned out – but that, of course, is another story.

Chapter Thirty-Four

Annie was delivered of a fine, full-term baby. She and her husband called the child John Arthur Brisker, and he was a joy to them both. Indeed, Brisker surprised his wife in his devotion to the child, and their love for the baby was a sort of bond between them. The two of them rubbed along, and in his way Brisker tried to please his wife. She was dutiful to him, and no more than that, although he continued to try and win her love. As before, however, he sometimes went out in the evening without saying where he went, and he still tried to impregnate her – as if he could not bear his failure to seed a child in her when another man had done so. Such a thing was part of her duty to him, but a circumstance one day, against every expectation, redeemed Brisker in the eyes of his wife.

Annie and her husband were walking along Walsall's historic High Street. Annie walked behind her husband, who strode along swinging his arms, sometimes raising his hat. Annie was distracted as she tried to keep up with him, and also by a street vendor who implored her to buy something or other. Behind her a horse was careering down the hill. Behind the animal a trap bounced and swayed; further back the trap's owner ran after it, shouting. People stood and watched. Brisker turned round. Annie, for whatever reason, did not notice that the animal would imminently knock her over.

A strange thing happened next; strange, one might think, as Mr Darwin would have thought it. If the business of an animal was to survive and breed, why then did Mr Brisker risk his life to throw his wife out of the way of the horse? In so doing he also saved the street vendor, although Brisker did not care about her. In the next moment the horse veered aside, but the corner of the trap caught Brisker and slammed him into the cobbles. Instantly, without fuss or drama, he gave up his life and lay dead. For all her estrangement from him, Annie was distraught. She tried madly to revive him and, inanely, made some attempt to staunch the bleeding from a wound in his scalp, until she was lifted up and supported. Hardly could Annie have told what happened next, but after a short time Brisker was carried into the Woolpack Inn, where Annie was given some brandy and whence she left for home without him. Her marriage had come to an end.

So it was, against expectation, that when George Bytheway was released Annie was waiting for him. Presently she became Mrs Bytheway, and he became master of Brisker's fine old home. Brisker might have resented this outcome, but if his angry spirit minded he did not intrude upon them – and nor did Bytheway think of him. Of course, people talked about them, but they, and their son, lived happily together, infamous but contented, and Bytheway, in particular, thought that he had been blessed.